MW01256712

HE STANDS
ALONE

BOOKS BY RANDY LEE EICKHOFF

THE ULSTER CYCLE

The Raid
The Feast
The Sorrows
The Destruction of the Inn
He Stands Alone

The Odyssey: A Modern Translation of Homer's Classic Tale

NOVELS

The Fourth Horseman
Bowie (with Leonard C. Lewis)
A Hand to Execute
The Gombeen Man
Fallon's Wake

NONFICTION

Exiled

A page from *The Book of Leinster,* a twelfth-century manuscript
that includes the tale of Cúchulainn's scythed chariot

HE STANDS ALONE

Randy Lee
Eickhoff

A TOM DOHERTY ASSOCIATES BOOK
NEW YORK

HE STANDS ALONE

Copyright © 2002 by Randy Lee Eickhoff

This book is printed on acid-free paper.

Frontispiece: TCD MS 1339.122.rle The Scythed Chariot, used with permission of The Board of Trinity College, Dublin.

Poems by Mícheál O'Ciardhi copyright © 2002 by Mícheál O'Ciardhi, used with permission of the author.

A Forge Book
Published by Tom Doherty Associates, LLC
175 Fifth Avenue
New York, NY 10010

www.tor.com

Forge® is a registered trademark of Tom Doherty Associates, LLC.

Library of Congress Cataloging-in-Publication Data

Eickhoff, Randy Lee.
    He stands alone / Randy Lee Eickhoff.
        p.   cm. — (Ulster cycle ; bk. 5)
    ISBN 0-312-87021-3
    1. Cuchulain (Legendary character)—Fiction. 2. Tales—Ulster (Northern Ireland and Ireland)—Adaptations. 3. Ulster (Northern Ireland and Ireland)—Fiction. 4. Epic literature, Irish—Adaptations. 5. Mythology, Celtic—Fiction. 6. Heroes—Fiction. I. Title.

PS3555.I23 H4 2002
813'.54—dc21

                                                                    2001054727

First Edition: March 2002

Printed in the United States of America

0   9   8   7   6   5   4   3   2   1

For Michael Carey

who has often walked
in the Otherworld
where all fear
to
tread.

And for Dianne,

who suggested
the title.

A Note of Thanks

I would be remiss if I did not acknowledge the presence of that wonderful Irish poet Mícheál O'Ciardhi for writing the poems that accompany the stories in this work.

2667   A mboi Galafas and ro cuala an guth n-ailgen a ndorus
         in durthigi
       Ised ro raidh: "Tair co luath, a modh Dé .i. a Galafas,
       Fo-geba anosa na hinganta nach fuair ridiri romad riam
       Nach fuighbi co bruindi in bratha."

Loargaireacht an tSoidhigh Naomhtha

Contents

Introduction 13

The Conception of Cúchulainn 21

The Story of Cúchulainn's Youth 37

Cúchulainn's Shield 65

Cúchulainn's Sword 67

The Training of Cúchulainn 71

The Wooing of Emer 91

The Elopement of Emer 133

The Death of Aife's Only Son 137

Cúchulainn and Fedelm 147

The Cattle Raid of Regamna 149

Cúchulainn and Senbecc 155

The Wasting Sickness of Cúchulainn

and The Only Jealousy of Emer 161

Appendix A: Structures in Ancient

Irish Poetry 207

Appendix B: The Healing Rivers 211

Appendix C: The Pangs of the

Ulstermen 213

Notes 219

Introduction

It would be difficult indeed to find a hero, legendary or otherwise, who has had as much impact on a culture as Cúchulainn in the Irish Ulster Cycle. Such was the enigmatic and charismatic appeal of the boy-warrior that his image and the heroic ideals he embodied were adopted by those fighting for Ireland's independence in 1916, when they realized that, like Cúchulainn, they stood alone against the formidable English army in a battle for independence. Sinn Féin, "Ourselves Alone," reflects that indefatigable spirit of the Irish who began the Republic's struggle toward freedom at the National Post Office in Dublin. The English brought in guns to destroy the post office and dislodge the rebels, necessitating the later rebuilding of the post office by the Irish. After they had finished, they placed one statue in the post office to commemorate the stand of the martyrs: a statue of Cúchulainn, who tied himself to a standing stone before he died so he could meet his enemies while still on his feet and alone, defiant against all odds. Such resoluteness makes the skin chill and pebble, as do the stories of this brave youth whose spirit is eternally bonded with the land and its people.

The stories of Cúchulainn have, unfortunately, undergone several distortions from the bardic tradition in which they existed for a thousand years or better before they were written down. The basic texts exist in *Leabhar* [*Lebor*] *Na hUidre* (the twelfth-century *Book of the Dun Cow*) and *Leabhar* [*Lebor*] *Laigneach* (the twelfth-century *Book of Leinster,* also known as *Lebar Na Núachongbála*). I have no doubt that during the transcription process the text was substantially altered in accordance with the scribe's pleasure and expectations. I base this conviction on a comparison of the tales themselves and on the information available about the culture of the Ancient Irish and speculations about their lifestyle and beliefs. The Anglo-Saxon epic *Beowulf* was altered by its monastic scribe in the much same way.

The stories of Cúchulainn compose the largest part of the Ulster, or Red Branch, Cycle, a group of sagas and romantic tales associated with traditional heroes who roamed the area that is now eastern Ulster, especially the present counties of Louth and Down. Emain Macha, the chief stronghold of the *Ulaid,* was destroyed around A.D. 332 and has been archaeologically identified as the grassy mound, close to Armagh, that is called Navan Fort (Centre).

This was the site where the powerful king Conchobor ruled, surrounding himself with a group of warrior-knights whose exploits suggest a literary kinship with some of the tales of the Arthurian knights of the Round Table. The exigence of the Red Branch tales, however, suggests that they preceded the Arthurian tales by quite a length of time.

In the Red Branch sagas, Ulster stands alone from the rest of Ireland, proud and haughty, stronger by far than the others thanks to her heroes Cúchulainn, Fergus Mac Roich, Loegaire Buadabach the Triumphant, Bricriu of the Poisoned Tongue, Conall Cernach, Sencha Mac Ailill, and Cathbad the Druid among others. Ulster's hereditary enemy, however, is Connacht, ruled by Ailill and his Amazonian wife, Maeve. Although queens were unknown to the Ancient Irish, many husbands bestowed upon their wives the same powers held by them. Consequently, Maeve is often referred to as Queen Maeve to distinguish the higher regard in which she was held by many (including herself). Maeve and Ailill, like Conchobor, are surrounded by a court of distinguished warriors at Rath Cruachan, their ancient capital.

These stories, whose earliest extant manuscripts date from the twelfth century to the fifteenth, are reflections of a much earlier period in Irish history; some were transcribed from originals written as early as the eighth century. The culture, however, was fairly similar to what prevailed in Ireland before the Christian intercession. The population was not united under one central government but existed instead in tribal unities or groups, each controlling its own district or province, known as *cóiced* (fifth), with Ulster occupying the north at Emain Macha and Connacht the west at Cruachan near the Shannon. The southeast of Ireland was controlled by the Laigin (Leinstermen), who were subdivided into the North and South, and in the southwest was Munster. Meath was carved out of the center after the provinces were united by the *Ard Rí,* or High Kings, in the second century after Christ. The famous Tara, symbol of the High King, was, however, unknown as the center of government until several centuries later.

Each *cóiced* was composed of smaller *tuathas,* or tribes, which were subdivided into even smaller groups, all bound together by fostering, the raising of another's child, a common practice that united two or more families as provided by the Brehon Laws, which were very explicit about how people and government must comport themselves. All owed allegiance to the *Rí Cóicid,* or provincial king.

The tales of this strange land, pagan and barbaric but replete with a splendor of civilization, are pastoral, although they lack the lyrical attention given to pastoral reflections by the later Romantics. Wealth was reflected in cattle and swine that roamed wide moors and deep forests. Exchanges and barters were made with the cow as the basic unit of value. Even slaves were given value in terms of cows (as seen in the Brehon Laws). It is highly significant that the national epic of Ireland is *Táin Bó Cuailngé* or *Cattle Raid of Cooley* (translated by the author as *The Raid*), which has as its central theme the attempt of the Connachtmen to carry away a famous bull that belonged to an Ulster chieftain.

These tales survived thanks to the poets who sang stories about the heroes and their accomplishments and wove those stories into a bardic tradition which demanded that practitioners be formally trained in the memorizing of certain tales and stories. That the poet was a most valued member of the king's household is reflected by the Brehon Laws, which set his pay as "twenty-one cows annually, plus enough pasture lands to feed them, plus two hounds and two horses."

The poetry of the Ancient Irish was highly complex and reflects a feeling and respect for nature. In essence, Ancient Irish poetry was based roughly on sound. That is, I admit, true of all poetry, but an oral tradition requires mnemonic devices such as alliteration, rhythm, and in some cases rhyme. Unfortunately, much of the documentation for the early poetic forms has been distorted by translators and transcribers, but the categories for this poetry are outlined in Appendix A.

The literature of the Ulster Cycle is, however, not exclusively poetry. Most of it is a mixture of poetry and prose, suggesting that the bard may have used a narrative to frame the poetry he believed most important. Curiously enough, the narratives now constitute the main body of early Celtic tradition. It is here, however, that the difficulty lies for the translator, who must not only translate but interpret that translation for his modern audience. A direct translation from Ancient Irish to modern English is, practically speaking, impossible. But the *intent* of the tale and teller may be given. An example of a Cúchulainn tale with as direct a translation as possible is given in Appendix B, but in this collection I have chosen to use the interpretive method instead. This method is, however, nothing new. It appears that, given the structural arrangement of the Ulster Cycle, the works were originally composed to be outlines of the tales, which the poets or bards would be required to "flesh out" in their telling. This method would offer the illusion of spontaneity as well as provide a means by which the individual could demonstrate his skills. I hasten to add, however, that not all scholars have accepted this theory.

As I said earlier, the bard was not self-appointed but had to earn his position through the memorization of a huge corpus of traditional stories and a demonstrated ability to compose new ones upon given subjects. The complex metrical devices are almost impossible to render into English. Consequently, I have tried to adapt the various types of poetry into a form familiar to the English reader.

Traditionally, the dwellings and households of the Ancient Irish were not especially elaborate but consisted of a large barn-like hall with couches around the sides and, in the middle, a fire pit and beer vat. Smoke found its way out through a hole in the roof. The doorways were probably closed by woven wattles during bad weather. Smaller houses and buildings formed a compound surrounded by sharpened pikes or stakes and heavy timbers raised against marauding tribes. A moat might be dug around the fortress as a further defense and, in some extreme cases, lakes would be established as well, forming *crannógs*.

The Ancient Celts' religion was based on worship of the sun and natural objects, especially trees and waters, but outside a skeletal pantheon of gods, little more is known of it. The Ancient Celts believed that another world existed in natural or artificial mounds (*sídhes*) and was inhabited by fairy folk endowed with eternal youth and beauty. These fairy folk sometimes slipped out of the Otherworld and took part in feuds and wars with mortals they favored. An ancient manuscript tells us these were the *dei terreni*, or Earth Gods, often referred to as the *Tuatha De Danann* (People of the Goddess Danu). Druids were those gifted with the "sight," which allowed them to communicate with the *sídhe*; consequently, the Druids became counselors to the kings.

A large number of the Cúchulainn tales are included in the epic *Táin Bó Cuailngé*, which I have already translated as *The Raid*. Consequently, I have elected to translate an obscure piece referred to as Recension III, which provides a shorter account of the great cattle raid. This particular recension is, however, in a fragmented state and is taken from two obscure manuscripts labeled Egerton 93 and H.2.17. Some names vacillate in spelling, for instance, Ailill and Oilill, but I have established consistency to avoid any confusion. Feargal Ó Béarra has suggested in *"Táin Bó Cuailngé:* Recension III," an article in *Emania,* no. 15 (1996), the bulletin of the Navan Research Group, that the work was actually "a reservoir of poachable material from which individual incidents or single lines could be taken over; a body of alternative material which could be used ... by the potential author/redactor." I see no reason to argue with that conclusion because when one compares this version to other accounts of the *Táin,* one finds huge gaps. My own theory is that Recension III was a training exercise for those studying to be bards, supplying the skeleton of the story, which each student would flesh out in recitation.

The stories in this collection are taken from a variety of sources, and in some instances I have combined two to complete a story in a semblance of the original. These combinations are, of course, conjectures, and I confess to taking certain liberties in order to clarify what I think was the text. My intent is to expose the modern reader to the ancient literature and the stories of a hero whose sense of honor was magnified by his humanism.

HE STANDS
ALONE

Brugh Na Bóinne: The Birth of Cú Chullainn

One warm August day
fifty birds landed on a fertile plain
and ate all that grew there.
The green ground was suddenly barren.
Then, a snow fell and a solitary house appeared
with a man and his woman in labor.
In the morning all these strange things disappeared.
Oh if only the world knew what was born into it that night
with the baby and the foals that fell against the door;
the something human and not human
that was conceived, not in *Deichtine* exactly,
not yet, how invisible particles of skin
began blowing through the dirt
and the sand once the snow had melted
only later to swirl into a form
she would recognize and learn to call, at times,
terror and *madness* and *love* and *tenderness* and *courage,*
something a mother could rock and feed,
and give life to for as long as the magic lasted.

Mícheál O'Ciardhi

The Conception
of Cúchulainn

The story of the birth of Cúchulainn exists in several recensions, one alleged to have been transcribed from the now lost *Book of Druimm Snechtai,* the others appearing in *Lebor Na hUidre* and in pieces in *The Book of Leinster.* Cúchulainn is the central character of the Ulster Cycle or, as it is sometimes referred to, the Heroic Cycle or the Red Branch Cycle. The period corresponds roughly to the beginning of the Christian era, although a lot of the tales can be found much earlier in the bardic tradition. This period was the golden age of Gaelic romance, which also included several stories and old-world sagas such as *Táin Bó Cuailngé,* the most important of the tales, and others concerned with Deirdre and the Sons of Uisneach, Conchobor's vision, the Battle of Rosnaree, and Conchobor's tragedy. The total number of tales is a question for scholarly argument; a hundred or more would be a conservative estimate.

Unfortunately, some of the works have been lost or "retold" so often that they bear little resemblance to the originals and scholars have a difficult time agreeing on which tale is most authentic.

The following retelling incorporates the two most common versions of the tale of Cúchulainn's birth (*Compert Con Culaind*). The first is taken from a *Lebor Na hUidre* manuscript, c. 1106; the second version comes from two recensions in Egerton 1782 (we no longer have the original, c. 1517).

fIRSC VERSION

Times had been hard at Emain Macha for the Red Branch but harder still for the farmers, who came complaining to the Great Hall to visit with the king, Conchobor Mac Nessa, about the difficulties of planting crops that became food for birds before taking root in the deeply rich ground of Ulster.

At last, weary of the complaints that kept coming his way, Conchobor elected to try to drive the birds away from Ulster.

"Let them take their food from Connacht for all I care," he grumbled angrily as he ordered his warriors to their chariots. " 'Tis a sad state when a man's own Druid can't do him the courtesy of taking care of such little annoyances."

Cathbad stared calmly back at his son the king and said, "Some little annoyances are the beginnings of major happenings. Take care that you don't confuse one with the other with your griping about grass and thistles."

Conchobor sighed and stared over at his champion, Fergus Mac Roich, and shook his head ruefully. "Have you ever gotten a word you could understand from a Druid?" he asked.

Fergus, whose head was pounding from his most recent ale-feast, which he insisted he had attended only to keep from breaking a *geis*, a taboo, that had been pronounced on him ("And a handy thing that is for a man who likes his drink," grumbled Nessa, his wife), winced from the sharp tongue lashed his way and said, "Druids don't have to speak in straight language. It's up to us to figure out what they say. Oh, my head!"

Cathbad smiled at this. "Not bad for one who thinks more with the sword between his legs than he does with the empty walnut shell on top of his shoulders."

"Don't press it, Druid," growled Fergus, shaking a thickly callused finger at him. "I'm in no mood to play fox and geese between you and your king."

"Quite right," Cathbad said quickly. He looked from under shaggy brows at Conchobor. "The truth of the matter is that there could be greater magic here than what you think. We can interpret the movings of the world but not control it."

"Well, then, let us ready nine chariots and draw a battle line with them and see if we can drive them from the lines," Conchobor said.

"Don't be surprised if you can't," Cathbad answered. "Your chariots may control the ground, but the birds have the air."

Conchobor grumbled and left to ready himself for his chariot. On the way, he encountered his daughter Deichtine, who was her father's charioteer. She smiled and batted her beautiful eyes at him, saying, "Well, handsome Father, and where are you off to now?"

"The birds," he said sourly, pausing to breathe in the sweet scent of clover that seemed to come from her. "They are causing more problems than you think. Than *I* think," he corrected. "We're going to try to drive them away from Emain Macha."

She shook her head. "Unless you can control the air, I don't think you'll have much luck," she said.

"You and Cathbad," Conchobor replied, shaking his head and moving past her. "Better if you were thinking about your wedding plans than worrying about the comings and goings of birds. Go ready the chariot."

When Conchobor and his chariots reached the plain before Emain Macha, they drew up in wonder at the barren ground

in front of them. Not a root, a leaf, or even so much as a blade
of grass stood on the ground, and the birds seemed to be gathered in the center, waiting for them.

"Arrogant bastards, aren't they?" Conchobor muttered to
his charioteer.

He glanced at the other chariots drawn up in a line on
either side of him. He waved a spear forward. "All right, warriors, let's try to send them back to Connacht. Or kill them. At
this point I don't care a hazelnut one way or the other. Just get
rid of them."

He looked to his immediate left, where the great champion
Conall Cernach waited, and to his right at the other champion,
Loegaire Buadabach. At the far end of the right wing, sour-
tongued Bricriu stood in his chariot. Conchobor took a deep
breath and waved the line forward.

The birds waited until the chariots were almost upon them,
then rose effortlessly and flew a short distance away, lighting
again, cawing and singing mockingly at the warriors they had
left behind.

"Enough!" Conchobor snapped. "It'll be a frozen day for
Manannan before I let a bird mock my coming and going. Kill
them!"

And with a mighty roar, the chariots rumbled forward.
Again, the birds waited for them, then rose tantalizingly into
the air as the warriors came within stone- and spear-cast range
of them and stayed just ahead of them as the warriors stubbornly chased them past Slíab Fúait, over Edmund, over Brega,
and slowly the warriors' mood melted and they became enchanted with the birds' flight and singing. They wondered at
the nine score birds, each score flying separately with silver
chains linking pairs together.

Little earthwork or fence or stone wall hampered them in
their chase. So it was that, toward evening, they found themselves a goodly distance from Emain Macha. Three birds broke

from the game and flew away toward Bruig na Bóinde. Then darkness slipped over the land, and with it came a great snow that further dampened Conchobor's spirits.

"Unyoke your chariots," he ordered, grumbling. "Conall, you and Bricriu see if you can find shelter for us this night before our balls freeze with the cold."

"Always me," Bricriu complained. "The others will gather around their fires, but here I am out in the cold, looking for a house where no self-respecting herder would put one." He shivered and drew his black cloak around his shoulders and glared malevolently at Conall, who seemed impervious to the cold. "And you don't feel it, do you?" he snapped waspishly.

"I feel it," Conall said calmly. "But I can't control it so I don't worry about it."

"Idiot," muttered Bricriu. Then a light seemed to shimmer and move behind the thick flakes in front of them. "A light!" Bricriu said, pointing.

"I see it," Conall said. " 'Tis a good grip you have on the obvious. Let's see if they have room for our party."

They moved up cautiously through the heavily falling snow until they came to a crude house made of logs, the chinks filled with grass. A happy couple greeted them when they knocked on the door and invited them in.

"Welcome! Welcome!" cried the master. "A foul night it's become and no place for a traveler. We don't have much, but you are welcome to what we have."

His bronzed face beamed at Bricriu and Conall. His shoulders strained the seams of his simple tunic while his wife gazed shyly up at them from red curls that tumbled down and around her fair white neck. Her belly was swollen, and it was apparent that she was near her time.

"Thank you," Conall said, "but we are not alone. We are the scouts for Conchobor, the king of the Red Branch, who waits for us."

"Bring him in! Bring him in!" cried the man. A soft golden glow seemed to circle his head. "There's always room for one more. Meanwhile, we shall work at making you all welcome. As I said, it isn't much, but you're surely welcome to it."

Conall nodded and stepped back outside, closing the door firmly behind him and Bricriu, who shivered and said, " 'Tis a small and narrow house not fit for the king. Or for any of us, for that matter. It didn't seem that he had enough food and clothing for us, and we'll probably have to sit around the fire in our wet clothes."

"Would you rather spend the night out here in the snow?" Conall asked.

Bricriu sighed and bit his lip. Even he could recognize that something was better than what they had, and when they told Conchobor what they had found, the king ordered that all move up close to the house, taking their chariots with them. They did not take their chariots inside the house—there wasn't room for them—but they did suddenly discover a storehouse door in front of them. They started to open it, but the man of the house came quickly between them and the door.

He smiled apologetically at Conchobor. "My wife has decided that this is the time to have our child," he said. "I beg that you allow her the privacy all women need at times like this."

"A child?" Deichtine said. She stepped forward and around the man of the house, placing her hand upon the latch. "Then she'll need the help of a woman, for certain. Besides"—she grinned at Bricriu—"if I help, there'll be just that much more room for the rest of you."

The man thanked her, and Deichtine entered the storeroom, firmly latching the door behind her.

"Well," the man said, rubbing his hands together. "There's a bit of food and drink for you and enough room that you'll be warm when it gets colder in the night."

"Argh," Bricriu grunted sourly, but the others ignored him and took the cups the host handed them, drinking and re-marking on the fine taste of the drink, and soon they were in good humor and singing their warrior songs.

Meanwhile, Deichtine helped the woman through her birth-ing. She delivered a son, and at the same time a mare that stood at the entrance of the house gave birth to two foals. The Red Branch warriors gave the two foals to the boy as a birth-gift for the lack of anything else. The mother was weak from the birth-ing, so Deichtine took the boy to her breast to nurse him as the men continued their party through the small hours of the night in celebration of the birth.

When morning came, however, the Ulstermen awoke to find themselves east of Bruig na Bóinde. Loegaire was the first to wipe the gummy night-tears from his eyes and look around in surprise. "Where's the house?" he yelped.

The others awoke instantly and stared around, bewildered.

"Magic!" Bricriu moaned. "I told you it was no good to stay here. Now here we are in the middle of a magic working and who knows what might be happening to us?"

"Shut your gob," Conall growled, climbing to his feet, his great sword in hand. He looked around carefully as Conchobor rose to stand beside him.

"Do you know where we are?" Conchobor asked.

"I know where we aren't," Conall said gruffly. He gestured with the sword. "No house, no birds, no host or his wife."

A child's cry came to them, and they turned and saw the newborn baby in Deichtine's arms. The two foals stood next to them.

"And what is this?" Conchobor asked.

Deichtine shook her head. "I do not know, Father," she said. "I awoke like you to find myself alone on the hillside with this child and the foals that were born to the mare last night."

"Well, at least the birds are gone," Conchobor said philosophically. He ordered that the chariots be yoked and that all return to Emain Macha.

They took the boy with them and raised him in the king's household until he approached early childhood. Then suddenly he took sick and died, and all in the house mourned his passing, for by now they had grown fond of the stripling.

Deichtine mourned his passing more than any other, for she had been a foster mother to the youth, and after she shed her tears, she found herself very thirsty. She went inside the Great Hall and there found a copper kettle, but every time she tried to drink from it, a tiny creature would leap from the liquid to her lips. Yet when she dropped it from her mouth, there was nothing to be seen and a great exhaustion seemed to come over her.

That night while she slept, a golden dream came to her, and from the depths of the dream a wondrous man spoke to her and said that she would bear his child. "It was I who brought you and the others to the Bruig na Bóinde, and it was I who made you welcome while my wife was giving birth. The child you nursed was my child, as is the one that I have placed within your belly. It will be a son, and you will call him Sétanta, and the foals shall be his when he is old enough to control them."

"Who are you?" she whispered, frightened by her dream.

He smiled at her and said, "I am Lugh Mac Eithliu. But this you already know, even though you do not know that you know it."

It wasn't long before all could see Deichtine was pregnant, yet she was still unmarried, and all the Ulstermen became concerned, for a rumor was circulating among them that it was a drunken Conchobor who had made her with child since his daughter used to sleep next to him.

Conchobor, however, pretended not to hear the words and

betrothed Deichtine to Sualdam Mac Roich, who owed him a great favor.

Now Deichtine was ashamed to go to her marriage bed with another's child in her belly, so when she came to Sualdam's bed she lay down and crushed the child within her until she was again like a virgin. Then she slept with her husband and was made pregnant by him and bore a son.

second version

Now it was that Deichtine, sister of Conchobor, he who was the king of Ulster, was betrothed to Sualdam Mac Roich, and much happiness was being planned at Emain Macha for her wedding.

On the morning of the event, however, Deichtine and fifty other maidens slipped away from the fortress and went on an elopement without any of the men from either Ulster or Connacht knowing a thing about it. Although the men tracked and cross-tracked in vain, they could find no trace of Conchobor's sister. For three years they searched, but not a scrap of dress was turned up or a single footprint that could be followed more than a short distance, where it seemed to disappear into thin air.

Deichtine and the maidens who attended her came to the plain in front of Emain Macha where they had been turned into the form of birds and, in that form, rapidly destroyed all the grass and seeds, leaving not so much as a single blade anywhere. The Ulstermen were greatly alarmed by this and harnessed nine chariots together to drive the birds away or, better yet, to hunt them down, for at this time bird hunting was considered great sport among the Red Branch. The hunting party consisted of Conchobor, Fergus Mac Roich, Amergin, Blai Briuga, and sharp-tongued Bricriu.

The birds, however, didn't wait for them to come within casting distance but rose and flew southward across Slíab Fúait, over the Ford of Letha and the Ford of Garach, and over the Plain of Gossa that lay between the men of Ross and the men of Arda.

Grimly the warriors followed the birds, determined to drive them from Emain Macha, but night fell before they got close enough to the birds to make a cast, and then they lost sight of the birds and were forced to make camp.

Wearily they unyoked their chariots while Fergus went to search out shelter for the men. It wasn't long before he came to a house newly built and found a married couple living quietly within.

"Come in! Come in!" cried the host, but Fergus shook his head and slapped his hands together. His nose twitched as he smelled rich ale, but there were others he had to contend with first.

"I would be happy to enter," he said, "but there are others who are with me, and it wouldn't be seemly if I were sheltered while they were left for the cold dew of the night."

"Then bring them in as well," the host said.

Fergus looked with misgivings at the small house, but he was too polite to refuse and went back to gather the others. All the men and horses went to the house with him, but when they stepped inside Fergus stopped in wonder. The small, crude house had become large and magnificent, and there was plenty of room for all within. He frowned, but the smell of ale was rich in his nostrils, so he went forward eagerly to the great vat of frothing ale that seemed to be waiting just for him.

Bricriu, however, had misgivings and went outside to check the area around the house. Faint strains of beautiful music came to him and, although he didn't know it was from the harp of Cnú Deireóil, he made his way along the trail the notes provided until he came to a great, fair, adorned house. He knocked on the door, and when it opened he found himself gazing upon the master himself.

"Come in, Bricriu," the master said. "Why do you insist on standing outside in the cold when it is warm within?"

At that moment a beautiful woman came up next to the master and smiled at Bricriu, saying, "Yes, indeed. You are very welcome."

Bricriu frowned and shook his head, trying to make sense of what had just happened to him. "Why does the woman welcome me more than the master?" he asked.

"Why, it is because of her that I welcome you," the man said. "But tell me: Is anyone missing from Emain Macha?"

Bricriu sighed and scrubbed his hand over his thick, oily black hair and pulled at his pouting lip with dirty fingers. "Yes," he said at last. "Yes, there are fifty maidens who have been missing for three years. Three years this very night," he added, scratching his head and trying to think back to see if that was indeed the case.

The man smiled. "Would you recognize them if you saw them again?" he asked.

Bricriu shrugged. "I might. Then again, I might not. The passing of three years or the sickness of three years may have made me ignorant or unable to recognize them."

The man laughed. "Well then, you still should try to see if you can recognize them. The fifty maidens you searched for are here in the house, and the woman by my side is none other than Deichtine. She and her maidens came from Emain Macha as a flock of birds in order to make the warriors come here."

The woman then gave a great purple cloak with a red border to Bricriu and asked him to take word back to the others about what he had found. While he was making his way back to the others, Bricriu began to think. "Now, if I was to tell Conchobor that I had found them, that wouldn't mean as much to him as if he had found them himself. So I won't tell him that I have found his sister and the other maidens who were with her. I'll just tell him that I have found a large house filled with beautiful women."

When Bricriu at last came to Conchobor and the king asked him the news, Bricriu drew upon his sourest face and said, "Well, what's it to you? I found a magnificent house, and within that house was a radiant queen and a noble man who was dear and lovable. A large company of fair and pure women served them. That was a generous and glittering household indeed."

"Is that true?" Conchobor asked, amused, for he knew well the wily and acid tongue of Bricriu. "Well, then, off you go back to that house, and since the master of the house is obviously a subject of mine for living in my land, tell him I desire that his wife come and sleep with me tonight."

"Ah, now," Bricriu said, embarrassed at the problem his reticence had made. "I have made my trip to that house. Let some other go in my place."

Fergus was the only one who agreed to deliver Conchobor's message when it was put to the others, and when he made his way to the house and spoke his message, the woman came away with him willingly. "It won't be the sleep the king thinks he'll be having," she warned him. "The pangs of childbirth are with me all ready."

Fergus sighed and draped a heavy arm around her shoulders, and when they came close to Conchobor, Fergus told the king that he should give her a respite, and Conchobor agreed. They all lay down for the night, and when they awoke they discovered that a baby boy had been delivered in the night and lay within the folds of Conchobor's own cloak.

Now Conchobor's sister Finnchoem had been traveling with them, and when Conchobor saw the child, he ordered Finnchoem to nurse him. Obediently, Finnchoem picked up the child, and her heart went out to the little boy and she said, "My heart loves this boy as if he was my own son, Conall."

"Well," Bricriu said grouchily, "there's that to be said for him, for there's little difference between them. That child is the son of your sister Deichtine, who has been absent with her fifty maidens from Emain Macha for nigh on three years now. There she is."

He pointed to where Deichtine lay exhausted upon her pallet.

Now the mysterious stranger who had been with Deichtine had been none other than Lugh Long-Arm of the Tuatha De Danann, and it was the order of Lugh that the child be named Sétanta, and it was this name that the child bore until the time came that he killed the hound of Culann the Smith and became known as Cúchulainn or the Hound of Culann.

But that was much later in the life of the baby; for now, the men of Ulster began to argue over which should bear the responsibility of being foster father to the boy. They almost came to blows before they asked Conchobor to make the decision and he glanced at where the boy lay gurgling happily in the arms of Finnchoem and said that she should be the one to raise him.

But Sencha protested this saying, "It is I, not Finnchoem, who should raise him, for I am strong and skillful. My deeds in combat are great, and I am known for being noble and nimble, learned and prudent. I have precedence in the king's presence and advise him before he speaks. I judge all the disputes that come before him. No one but Conchobor would make a better foster father than I would."

Blai Briuga snorted with disgust and rose, throwing his head back and looking down through slitted eyes at Sencha. "No, let me foster him. He'll not come to any harm or neglect with me at his side. My household is large enough to feed all the men of Ireland for an entire week, and none go away from my house soured by my decisions. Let my claim be settled by Conchobor."

Fergus shook his head in wrath. "Have you no respect for the child? Bittering and barking like this! I'm concerned about the child. I will foster him. No one can match me in rank or riches or in courage, and none can meet my skill at arms. My honor alone makes me the ideal foster father. I am the scourge of the strong and the savior of the weak."

Amergin laughed and said, "Well, then, don't turn away until I have my words. I am worthy enough to bring up a king! My deeds are well-known and my wisdom and wealth without challenge. Others come from far around to hear my eloquence and my open-minded decisions, and my courage and the rank of my family are without question. If I weren't already a prince, my poetry would surely make me one. And as for my strength, why there isn't a chariot chieftain around I couldn't kill if I put my mind to it. I look up to no one but the king himself."

Conchobor shook his head. "Quit this nattering," he said. "Finnchoem will look after the boy until we reach Emain Macha. There, Morann the Judge will make the decision as to who shall be the foster father. I have spoken."

With a great deal of grumbling and darting, deadly eyes, they made ready to return to Emain Macha, where Morann delivered his judgment.

"The boy should be given to Conchobor, for he is related to Finnchoem. Sencha shall teach him eloquence and oratory. Blai Briuga shall provide for him. Fergus will take him on his knee and teach him weapons. Amergin will be his teacher, while Conall Cernach shall be his foster brother. Finnchoem shall nurse him. And so all will have a part in raising him to become a chariot chief, prince, and sage. This boy will be loved by many and will settle your trials of honor and win many battles and ford fights."

And so he was given to Amergin and Finnchoem and brought up at Dun Imrith on the Muirthemne Plain.

Sétanta's Reply to Culann:
The Naming of Cú Chulainn

So I killed the beast.
He came running at me, so I took him
by the shoulders and the hindquarters
and dashed his head against a stone.
Wouldn't you, if you could?
Weren't we both trained from birth
to kill or to be killed? Wasn't he
three times larger than myself
and all the doors of the house locked against me?
I am sorry, but how can I repay you
when all that I own is a name? And of what worth is that?
Isn't everyone on this wide earth wrong, misplaced, or ill-
devised?
How could what is inside ever hope to be captured or known
fully?
Isn't the soul always shifting?
From now on, let *me* guard what you possess,
everything you love that loves you in return.
I, who could destroy this whole village
and everyone in it, will willingly be your dog.
I will howl at the night. I will snuff out
whatever intrudes or frightens anyone in your family.
I will be the form fear takes
in the unconscious heads of your drowsing enemies,
a prince yes, but not a ruler—a servant.
A name is an easy thing to change,
a heart isn't.

                                        Mícheál O'Ciardhi

The Story of Cúchulainn's Youth

This story also appears in my book *The Raid*. It forms, however, a cohesive part of the story of Cúchulainn leading up to the famous *Cattle Raid of Cooley* and must, therefore, appear at this point. *The Story of Cúchulainn's Youth* is actually a compilation of many smaller stories drawn from various sources, such as *The Book of Leinster, The Yellow Book of Lecan, Lebor Na hUidre,* the Edinburgh manuscript, and Rawlinson B in Oxford.

SERVANTS MOVED QUIETLY AMONG THE advisers in Ailill's tent, serving fresh and salted pork to those reclining upon cushions, along with fish seasoned with cumin and honey-baked salmon. Ale and mead flowed freely, but some took advantage of wine that had been traded from ships.

Fergus settled himself comfortably. He spat into the fire and leaned back on his elbows upon the rug that had been laid for his comfort. A servant handed him a jeweled cup of spiced wine. He sighed happily: the whole evening lay before him like a meadow. He took a long drink, sighed, belched, smacked his lips with relish, and began:

"Cúchulainn was raised by his father, Sualdam Mac Roich, and mother, Deichtine, Conchobor's sister, in their house of oak on the high, grassy plains of Muirthemne. While still a small boy, he heard stories about the one-hundred-fifty-boy boy-troop in Emain. It has always been so, you know. Conchobor spends one-third of his day watching the boys at play, one-third in which he plays *fidchell*[1] (he cheats, you know, moving his men when you look away and then pretending he has yet to move when you look back. A trifle, perhaps, but a character fault, nonetheless), and another third drinking strong ale until sleep comes upon him. Ah, Conchobor!" He sighed. "I miss the *fidchell* board and those days! Good days they were, lazing in the sun beneath the ash tree at the end of the boys' playing field. Honeybees, the soft wind—"

"I hope," Maeve said, interrupting his meditation, "that you do not miss them too much. It would not be good for you if we thought you were deliberately leading us away from Ulster."

Fergus fixed a strong eye upon Maeve. "Do not come upon me with your queenly ways, Maeve! I was a king long before Ailill consented to let you pretend to rule. Aye! Don't be babbling your lips with idle threats! Only a horn blow keeps my warriors from falling upon your Connacht petty prissies, and then what army you'd have left wouldn't be enough to empty your piss pot!"

Maeve started up, but Ailill raised his hand, pain showing between his eyes. "Enough of this bickering! If you wish to stay in the council of warriors, then mind your place," he said to Maeve. He ignored her as she pressed her lips tightly together and leaned back upon her cushions. "And you, Fergus! Ulster warriors are surely better men than to rise to a woman's quarreling words! Get on with your story, man!"

"No greater warrior lives in Ireland than Conchobor," Fergus said slowly, enjoying the sparks coming from Maeve's eyes, for he knew that Conchobor had once been her husband, but it had not been Maeve who had left him despite the Connacht woman's pretense. "And I say this even though he forced me into exile ten blue winters ago. Now, where was I? Oh yes.

"One day, Cúchulainn, lonely with no other children to play with, begged his mother to allow him to travel to Emain Macha and join the boy-troop there.

" 'You can't go that far,' Deichtine said. 'The way is far too dangerous. Wait for the new moon. Some Ulster warriors will undoubtedly be traveling there then, and you may go with them if you wish.'

" 'I cannot wait that long,' Cúchulainn said impatiently. 'Please: point the direction toward Emain Macha.'

" 'You have to travel to the north,' his mother said at last in exasperation. 'But the road is long and hard, and Slíab Fúait is between here and there. You must be very careful when you travel through there as there are many in that area who do not take well to strangers.'

" 'I still will try it,' Cúchulainn answered stubbornly.

"And so he left the oaken home of his parents armed with only a toy shield made from sticks woven together, toy javelin, and his hurling stick and ball. As he traveled, he played a game by throwing the javelin high in front of him and running to catch it before it struck the ground.

"At last, he came to Emain Macha, high on a hill and surrounded by a deep ditch topped by a palisade of timber. There he saw the boy-troop playing in the field. Excitement filled him so that he forgot himself and ran up to Conchobor's boys without asking for their pledge of safety. He did not know that no one, not even Conchobor or myself, went onto the boys' playing field without first requesting a promise of safety from them. That is the tradition of the boy-troop, you see. One started by

Conchobor himself. The pledge teaches respect and manners, you see.

" 'I can see that this youth comes from Ulster, but yet he challenges us by coming among us without permission. He should know better,' said Follamin, Conchobor's son.

"The boys on the field shouted warnings at Cúchulainn, but he ignored them and continued making his path toward them. They threw one hundred fifty javelins at him, but he deflected them with his stick shield. Then they drove their hurling balls at him, but he caught them all upon his chest. They threw their hurling sticks at him, but he eluded every one of them except for those few that he pulled down as they flew past, anger building in him.

"It was now that we saw the man beneath the boy's skin." Fergus's voice became quiet. The others strained forward, trying to catch his words before he spoke them. "The warp-spasm, terrible to behold, came upon him. Each hair seemed hammered down like a spike into his head, the end of each tipped with a fire-spark that burned like brimstone. One eye squeezed shut like the eye of a needle, while the other opened as wide as a goblet's mouth. His lips peeled back to his eyeteeth until his gullet showed, and his jaws gaped wide to his ears. Then the hero-halo rose up in a shimmering cloud from the crown of his head, and he charged the boys although they greatly outnumbered him. The boys hesitated at the spectacle, then Badb whispered in their ears and they fled in terror from him.

"He knocked fifty of them unconscious to the ground before they got to the gate of Emain. Nine of them flew past Conchobor and myself where we played *fidchell* as if they had wings upon their feet. But he leaped after them over the *fidchell* board, knocking the pieces to the grass. Conchobor caught his wrist as he flew by, pulling him around, but such was his fury that even Conchobor could scarce hold him. I leaped over and grabbed his other arm, holding with all my strength against the rage of the youth. Slowly the warp-spasm left him.

" 'You have damaged some of these boys badly,' Conchobor said sternly when the youth reappeared.

"He pulled free from Conchobor's grasp, saying, 'I am in the right, friend Conchobor. I left my home and my mother and father to join with them, but they did not accept me. They threw their javelins and hurling balls and hurling sticks at me. They have only received what they sought to give me.'

" 'Who are your parents? What do they call you?' demanded Conchobor.

" 'I am Sétanta, son of Sualdam and your sister Deichtine,' the boy answered. 'I did not expect to be treated in this manner when I came here. The boys' hospitality is lacking in manners.'

" 'Why didn't you place yourself under protection from the boys by asking them to receive you?' Conchobor asked curiously.

" 'I did not know that was the way things were done here,' said Cúchulainn. He threw his long hair back from his eyes and held himself proudly erect, treating Conchobor as a warrior would. 'But now, I ask for your protection and hospitality.'

" 'Very well,' said Conchobor, trying to repress a smile. 'You may have it.'

"Cúchulainn turned to chase after the boys through the house, but Conchobor again stayed him.

" 'What do you plan on doing to them now?' he asked.

"Cúchulainn gave him a puzzled look. 'Why, I plan to offer them my protection,' he said.

" 'I see,' Conchobor said. His eyes became hard, and when they looked like gray stones, no warrior would dare to ignore his words. 'Perhaps it would be wise for you to offer it here and now. Just in case something should go wrong when you talk with them. Those boys, too, are under my protection.'

" 'I promise,' Cúchulainn said promptly, giving his word.

"And he kept it when all of us went out to the playing field, where the foster mothers and fathers of the boys whom Cúchulainn had struck down were helping the wounded boys to their feet."

Fergus took another glass of wine to ease the dryness in his throat from talking. The others waited impatiently, seeing that he had more to tell them about the warrior they were facing. At last, he began again:

"Once, when he was a young boy, he could not sleep at all in Emain Macha. Concerned over his welfare, Conchobor called Cúchulainn, red-eyed and irritable, to him. " 'Tell me, Cúchulainn, why is it that you cannot sleep here in Emain Macha?' he asked.

" 'I must have the same level under both my feet and my head,' he answered. 'Otherwise, I cannot sleep.'

"So Conchobor arranged for two blocks of stone to be sized and cut and dressed for Cúchulainn and a special bed to be built between them for him.

"Tired, Cúchulainn lay down and immediately fell into a deep sleep, for it had been a long time since he had last slept. After a while a man attendant was sent in to awaken him. When the man touched him, Cúchulainn lashed out blindly at him, striking him in the forehead with his fist, driving his forehead back into his brainpan. He threw his arm aside to push himself erect and knocked the stone block flat with his arm."

"That was a warrior's fist. A born-warrior's arm," Ailill mused. Pain flickered over his face. He farted, and the hard lines relaxed. He sighed in relief.

"Yes," Fergus answered, leaning back from the smell rising from Ailill's cushions. He absently scratched his chest through his tunic with a horny thumb. "But it was a lesson well learned, for from that time on no one has awakened him. He is left to awaken by himself. It is a *geis* that all must obey.

"Another time when he was playing ball in the playing field

east of Emain, he defeated all one hundred fifty boys who had challenged him. He always won," Fergus continued. He twirled his wineglass between thick, callused fingers. "I watched him work: every time they laid a hand upon him, he would work with his fist, knocking them senseless fifty at a time. When the rest of the Red Branch (myself included, I admit, and Conchobor himself) saw what he had done, they rose in fury against him. He ran and hid under Conchobor's bed. We should have left him there, but never had the boy-troop been so destroyed!

In anger, we ran after him. When we came into the room, he suddenly straightened up from under the bed, lifting it high and heaving it into thirty warriors, knocking them to the floor, stunning them. The others circled him and bore him back by sheer numbers. But by then his fury had cooled us and no punishment was given him, for we knew that he had been the intended victim of the boy-troop. At last Conchobor and I made a peace between the boy-troop and Cúchulainn. We had to do this, you see. Otherwise . . ." Fergus shrugged, leaving the rest unspoken.

With a sudden movement he took another drink of wine, draining his cup, then held it out to a servant to refill. He sighed and stretched his feet out to the fire. He was getting old, and his feet needed to be warmed now and then. He sighed again and scratched his head, frowning as his fingers slid through oily hair. He sniffed the ends of them and grimaced and made a note to have his bondmaids wash it.

"Well?" Maeve said impatiently. "Is that it?" She shook her head, her lips curling in derision. "It appears that this is only a child's tale, a fantasy of a boy who would be a warrior."

Fergus laughed. He reclaimed his cup from the bondmaid and took a large drink of wine, swallowing it in installments. "You know little of what makes a warrior. Much more than playing a woman's game."

She flushed. "I have had many dealings with warriors," she began heatedly, but Ailill interrupted her.

"Yes, yes, yes, yes! But for now, be quiet! We are not here to listen to your bed boasts," he said sternly. "Go on with your story, Fergus."

Fergus nodded, took another drink, and stared deeply into the past, rolling his tongue along his teeth, remembering.

"Then, there was the time when Eogan Mac Druthact challenged all of Ulster to a battle. While Cúchulainn slept, the Red Branch answered Mac Druthact's challenge. They were ill prepared for this and soundly beaten. Conchobor and his son Cúscraid Menn Macha, the One Who Stammers, were left for dead with other warriors heaped around them. The wailing of the warriors and the women over the lost battle woke Cúchulainn. He stretched, throwing his arms out, and cracked two stones beside him. Bricriu of the Bitter Tongue saw this, so it is true," Fergus added. "He rose and went out to Emain's gate, where he met me, covered with wounds." Absently, he ran a thick forefinger down a ridged scar on his heavily muscled forearm.

" 'I am sorry about your wounds. May God help you, friend Fergus,' he said. He looked around, concern frowning from his brow. 'Where is Conchobor?'

" 'I don't know,' I answered, feeling faint from my wounds. I wanted a healer then, and not to spend idle time chatting with a youth.

"So Cúchulainn left me and went out into the black night, turning his steps toward the slaughter field. A *bocánach* flew across the silver sickle moon, cackling. I shuddered as I looked back upon the ground I had just left, black from blood soaking into the earth. Cúchulainn seemed not to notice the ground or smell the fetid stench rising like mist around him. The moans of the dying rose around him like notes from a *cruitire,* a black harper. I thought I saw flames lick in the distance from the fire breath of a *péist,* but I was feeling faint from my wounds, for

I am sure now that the *Súil Bhalair,* the Eye of Balor, had fallen upon me during the fighting. Cúchulainn chanced upon a half-headed man bearing half a corpse upon his back.

" 'Help me, Cúchulainn,' the man said. 'I am hurt and carry half of my brother upon my back. Carry it for me awhile.'

" 'No,' answered Cúchulainn.

"He meant to speak more, but the man threw his brother's corpse at Cúchulainn. He dodged the corpse and grappled with the man. They strained against each other, sinews snapping with their efforts, and then the wounded man threw Cúchulainn to the ground.

"I watched this from afar, surprised that a wounded man could best Cúchulainn, but suddenly I heard a voice: the Badb calling from a pile of corpses: ' 'Tis a poor warrior who lies down at the feet of a ghost!' Whereupon Cúchulainn rose with his hurling stick in his hand and struck the half-head from the man's body, driving it like a hurling ball across the plain of battle. And then I knew the man to be an *aithech,* a churl of the Fomorians, lords of darkness and death.

" 'Conchobor!' Cúchulainn yelled, his voice booming across the plain. 'Are you on this field of battle?'

"Faintly, Conchobor answered. He cried out again, but I could not hear his words. Cúchulainn followed the sound of his voice and finally discovered him lying in a trench with earth piled up around him, hiding him in its breastworks.

" 'Why do you walk among the dead on this slaughter field?' Conchobor asked painfully. 'Are you trying to learn mortal terror?'

"Cúchulainn did not answer but reached down and pulled him from the ditch. Conchobor gasped with pain as the young boy lifted him from that breastwork of earth. Six of the strongest Ulstermen could not have dragged him from that ditch, but Cúchulainn did it with ease. He lifted Conchobor to his shoulders, and Conchobor noted an old *seantán* standing against the dark line of the woods a short distance away and said: 'Take me to that shack and light a fire therein for me.'

"And Cúchulainn obeyed, kindling a great fire in the hearth for him. He settled Conchobor before the fire, and Conchobor sighed with pleasure, for he had grown very cold lying in the ditch with Badb's breath blowing over him, waiting for someone to pull him free.

" 'Ah,' he said. 'Now, if only I had some cooked pork I might find some life within me.'

" 'Then I shall go and get one for you,' Cúchulainn said simply.

"And he left the shack and entered the forest that stood behind the house, searching for a pig among the bramble thickets. He came upon a hard-faced man by a cooking pit where he roasted a boar while bearing his weapons in his huge hand.

"He struck out at Cúchulainn, but he was no match for the youth. Cúchulainn dodged his first stab, then attacked and killed him easily, driving his fist into the man's brainpan, then used the man's sword to take his head as well as the boar back to Conchobor.

"Conchobor ate the entire boar, then rested for a bit, warming his wounds before the fire. At last he told Cúchulainn that he was ready to return home. On the way back, they found Cúscraid, Conchobor's son, heavy with wounds. Cúchulainn did not pause but lifted Cúscraid to his back as well and carried both him and his father back to Emain Macha."

Fergus hawked and spat. He wiped his lips with the back of his hand and combed the snarls from his beard with his fingers, thinking. At last, he smiled.

"I remember another time if you all are not too tired from hearing about Cúchulainn's feats," he said. He glanced around the circle and saw with satisfaction that none expressed a desire for him to remain silent. He grinned and took another sip of wine before beginning.

"Once when the Ulstermen were in their pangs[2]—this affliction was borne by the men only, not the women or children or anyone not from Ulster, which excluded Cúchulainn and his father. No one dared to spill an Ulsterman's blood while they were suffering from their pangs, for if one did, why then, the Curse of Sinrith Mac Imbaith would fasten itself upon that one and he would begin to grow old before his time or else die shortly after.

"As it happened, twenty-seven raiders came from the Faichi Islands and broke through the rear gate while we lay helpless with our pangs. The women began screaming as the raiders came upon them, stripping their clothing from them and assaulting them. Naked bodies rolled in the dust, firelight flickering redly from the sweating bodies. Our women fought, but they were no match for the strength of the raiders. The boy-troop heard their screams from their playing field and raced to help them. But when the boy-troop saw those dark men, they ran away. All but Cúchulainn. He did not hesitate but attacked them with throwing stones from his sling and his hurling stick. He killed nine of them, although he suffered more than fifty wounds himself from their swords and battle-axes. When the raiders saw he was still determined to fight, they fled for their lives. And remember: this was all before he was five years old. Small wonder, then, that a man would have such little trouble cutting off the heads of our four warriors, right?"

"Yes," Conall Cernach, one of the listeners, answered. "Yes, we know about the boy, those of us who have followed Fergus into exile. I knew him better than most, for I fostered him. It wasn't long after these deeds that he performed yet another."

While Fergus replenished himself with more wine, Conall took on the job as *seanchai,* the storyteller.

"One day Culann the Smith decided it was time to entertain Conchobor. You have to remember that, under the rules of hospitality, it is only natural and good for each person to entertain his king sometime after Samhain. But Culann had no land or property with which to sponsor the type of feast usually given to Conchobor (he had only what he could earn with his tongs and hammer, although a wheelwright is highly valued among the people), so he was forced to ask Conchobor not to bring too many of his *laochra* with him. Conchobor knew this and, thinking kindly of Culann, left with only fifty chariots of his best champions to accompany him. But before he left, he went by way of the playing field to say good-bye to the boys. When he arrived, he saw that Cúchulainn was playing ball against all one hundred fifty of the boys and beating them.

"When they played for the goal, Cúchulainn peppered the goal with his shots and all were helpless to stop him. When it came their turn to shoot against Cúchulainn, he turned all their shots aside. When they tried to wrestle with him, he pinned all hundred fifty, and when they thought to play the stripping game with him, he left them naked while not one could even pluck the brooch that held his cloak to his shoulder.

"Conchobor was truly surprised at this and asked the other boys if they thought there would remain the same differences between their abilities once all reached manhood. All claimed sheepishly that the differences would remain the same, so Conchobor impulsively invited Cúchulainn to come with him to Culann's feast.

" 'I would like to finish this game, friend Conchobor. You go ahead, and I will follow when I am finished,' Cúchulainn said.

"So Conchobor went on ahead, but by the time he arrived at Culann's house, he had forgotten that he had told Cúchulainn to come after him after the boy-troop had finished the game.

" 'Are you expecting anyone else to come?' Culann asked. 'I inquire only for politeness, for I have a savage hound that takes three chains to hold him back with three men on each

chain. I use him to guard my house and will release him outside
the gate to guard us while we feast.'

" 'No,' Conchobor said absently, his eye following a round-
rumped bondmaid whose saucy eyes spoke bed invitations. 'No
one is following me.'

" 'Good,' Culann said. 'Then release the hound to guard
our cattle and stock,' he ordered his servants. 'Be certain that
you close the gate after, though.'

"The servants did as they were told. Later, when the boy
came up the road, the savage hound spied him and set upon
him, baying his hunting call, slobber dripping from his huge
fangs, madness gleaming from his eyes. But Cúchulainn was
still playing with his hurling stick and threw his hurling ball
up into the air and stroked it, hurling his javelin after it and
catching both before they hit the ground.

Conchobor and his company heard the savage growls of the
hound and rushed to the parapets to see what was happening.
When they saw the hound nearly upon the boy, they became
horrified, but there was nothing for them to do, for they were
not able to reach the boy in time to keep the hound from him.
The hound leaped for his throat, but Cúchulainn tossed his stick
and ball aside and caught the hound by its throat beneath its
shaggy head; squeezing the apple flat with one hand and grasp-
ing its back through its thick fur with the other, he smashed it
against the nearest pillar of the house with such force that its
limbs leaped from their sockets. This I saw, although some
claimed that he had smashed his hurling ball down through its
mouth with his hurling stick, tearing its guts out its anus. But
I tell you that it happened the way I saw: he simply smashed
the hound against the pillar as if it were only a mouse from the
field.

"The Ulstermen threw open Culann's gates and rushed out
to greet him. Some of the warriors leaped from the parapet, so
excited were they at this exhibition of strength. Together, they

raised him to their shoulders and carried him in triumph to Conchobor, cheering that the son of the king's sister had escaped harm or death.

"But Culann was not happy at the outcome, although he remembered the rules of hospitality and made Cúchulainn welcome.

" 'For your mother's sake, you are welcome,' he said. He bowed to Conchobor. 'I am sorry that my feast has turned out so badly. Now my life is wasted and my household is like a wasteland since my hound has been taken away. He meant nothing to you, but he guarded my property and my honor and kept my stock from being taken from me by rogues. Alas! Now we shall be defenseless, for I cannot afford the *curadh* to guard my property.'

" 'I am sorry for causing you grief,' Cúchulainn said magnanimously. 'I will raise a pup for you from the same pack that fostered your hound. And until that hound ages enough to become the guard for your property, I will be your hound and guard your property and all of the Muirthemne Plain.'

"These were strong words and from the mouth of another youth would have been taken for boasting and therefore frivolous. But Cúchulainn was sincere and all there could see his sincerity and Culann agreed to his terms.

" 'Then your name shall become Cúchulainn, the Hound of Culann,' Cathbad the Druid said to the youth.

" 'I prefer my own name, Sétanta,' Cúchulainn said, frowning at the Druid. 'Why is it that Druids always want to change a person's name?'

" 'A child bears a child's name until he becomes man enough to carve out his own with his deeds,' Cathbad said. 'Sétanta will remain unknown, for it is a name given by a mother, while Cúchulainn will live forever in the memory of men,' Cathbad replied.

" 'Then that is a good name, indeed,' Cúchulainn said. And

from that day on he was called by his new name.

"So is it any wonder that a boy who could do this in his sixth year could do what he did today to our men while seventeen?" Conall Cernach asked the gathering.

"There was yet another deed," Fiacha Mac Fir Febe said, taking on the role of storyteller. "Not long after this happened, Cathbad the Druid was staying with Conchobor Mac Nessa, his son, while a hundred studious men were at his feet, learning the lore of the Druids from him. (This was always the number that Cathbad taught: when one left, he made room for another.)

"One day during their lessons, a student asked him how that day would bring luck. (As you all know, each day is made for certain things, and these things the wise Druids are privy to.) Cathbad answered by saying any warrior who took up arms for the first time that day would find his name enduring in Ireland forever as a symbol of mighty acts and deeds.

"Cúchulainn overheard Cathbad's words and straightaway went to Conchobor to claim his weapons. When Conchobor asked him by what authority he claimed his weapons, he said, 'My friend Cathbad.' "

Fiacha paused, frowning. "That's the trouble with Druids. Always speaking in vagaries," he said.

"They call it wisdom," Ailill said impatiently. "Go on. Or else this story will take the entire night."

Fiacha shrugged and continued. " 'I see,' Conchobor said. Knowing Cathbad to be wise and able to see down the days yet to come, Conchobor gave the boy a shield and spear. But when Cúchulainn tried these out, they broke from his strength. One by one Conchobor gave Cúchulainn set after set of the weapons that he kept for the warriors who might break theirs, but each set fell apart in Cúchulainn's hands. At last Conchobor gave Cúchulainn his own weapons, and when Cúchulainn discovered how fine these weapons were and how strong they remained in his hands, he saluted Conchobor with his own weapons and pledged himself to him.

"At this moment, Cathbad entered the room and saw Cúchulainn holding his new weapons.

" 'Is this boy newly armed?' Cathbad asked in alarm.

" 'He is,' Conchobor answered proudly. 'He carries my own weapons, for none other are worthy of him.'

" 'Then his mother will know sorrow,' Cathbad said, shaking his head.

" 'What?' Conchobor exclaimed. 'Did you not send him to me to receive his arms?'

" 'I did not,' Cathbad said.

"Conchobor turned in anger to Cúchulainn. 'Devil, why did you lie to me?' His lips were white with his anger, and his shoulders and legs trembled from his fury.

" 'But I did not lie to you, king of warriors,' Cúchulainn said. 'I overheard him in his instruction with his students when one of them asked him what this day would bring. This was south of Emain Macha,' he said, and Cathbad nodded when Conchobor looked at him for confirmation, signifying that it was so. 'It was then that I came to you.'

" 'That is true,' Cathbad said, 'but I think you were so eager to receive your arms that you did not listen to what else I said: that he who does arm himself for the first time today will certainly achieve fame and greatness, but his life will be very short. Very short, indeed.'

"Others might have flinched from this news, but not Cúchulainn. He grinned at Cathbad and said, 'Well, then, that is a fair bargain. I will accept that. I will be content even if I have only one day left on earth. For that is the only immortality that we are given.'

"The next day, the same student asked Cathbad what luck that day would bring for someone.

" 'Who mounts his first chariot today will find his name living forever in Ireland,' Cathbad said.

"And Cúchulainn overheard this, too, and went to Conchobor saying, 'Friend Conchobor, I claim my right for a chariot!'

"And Conchobor, seeing the spirit of the boy, weakened and gave him a chariot. Cúchulainn clapped his hands between the shafts of the chariot, and the spars broke cleanly at his touch. He tested twelve other chariots in this same manner until, at last, Conchobor gave him his own chariot to use. That one survived the test. Cúchulainn gleefully mounted the chariot beside Conchobor's own charioteer, Ibar by name, who turned the chariot around the courtyard with its right side to the sun to bring luck to Cúchulainn.

"When he had finished making the rounds, Ibar said to Cúchulainn, 'You may step down now.'

"At this, Cúchulainn laughed. 'You may think your horses are precious,' he said to Ibar. 'But I am even more valuable. Take me around Emain Macha now.'

"Reluctantly, Ibar drove the chariot through the gate and down the road at Cúchulainn's urging to where the boy-troop practiced on their playing field. When they saw Cúchulainn in the chariot, they all cheered him and Cúchulainn told Ibar: 'Whip the horses forward.'

" 'To where?' Ibar asked.

" 'Wherever the road takes us,' Cúchulainn answered.

"Amused by now at the young upstart, Ibar struck up the horses, pointing their noses down the road. Soon they came to Slíab Fúait. This was the place that had fallen to Conall Cernach to guard on that day. It was the province boundary where each of Ulster's warriors, those of the Red Branch, was supposed to care for and make welcome all men who came that way with poetry upon their lips and to fight with any others who tried to cross the boundary. But it was the place where many evil men came as well, for it was the main road to the Red Branch.

Conall was there to keep Emain Macha safe from surprise. To be chosen as that guard was a great honor.

"When Cúchulainn arrived in his new chariot, Conall greeted him with the words that one normally used in greeting his friends. 'May you be rich in the future,' Conall said. 'May your victories be many and your triumphs great.'

"Cúchulainn stepped down from his chariot and grinned at Conall. 'Friend Conall,' he said. 'Go back to the fort and leave me here to watch for you.'

" 'Well, you might do for looking after men whose lips drip poetry, but you are still too young to challenge warriors,' he teased. 'And,' he added, 'you are lacking the niceties in speech by which friends greet each other. You are not fully a warrior yet.'

"Cúchulainn felt a moment's annoyance but quickly pushed down the irritation. 'Well said, friend Conall! And I apologize if my words were too eager in greeting. But I may never have a chance to challenge warriors. At least,' he added, 'not for a long while. Still, there is a chance, a chance. Let's wander down to Loch Echtra, where warriors often camp by the lake.'

"The day was hot, and the thought of a cool hour or two spent by the shores of the lake appealed to Conall. He grinned at Cúchulainn. 'Now there is a happy thought,' he agreed.

"They set off in their chariots, Cúchulainn in his while Conall put his horses next to those of Cúchulainn. Cúchulainn played with his sling, bouncing stones off stones, off trees, knocking a hornet's nest from an oak, a knob off a blackthorn. Suddenly, Cúchulainn whirled his sling overhead and dashed a stone against the shaft of Conall Cernach's chariot, smashing it. Conall pulled hard on his reins to keep the startled horses from running away. He looked sternly over at the youth. 'Why did you break the shaft of my chariot with that stone, boy?' he asked dangerously. Anger glinted from his eyes, but Cúchulainn did not flinch from them.

" 'To test my hand and aim,' he answered. He gestured toward Conall's broken chariot. 'I am sorry that you will have to return to Emain Macha now, friend Conall, but you are fairly useless with that chariot. Go on back and leave me here in your place as guard.'

"For a moment, Conall was tempted to take the boy's chariot from him, but something about Cúchulainn made him withhold the sharp retort threatening to erupt from his lips. 'If I must, I must,' Conall growled.

"While Cúchulainn continued on with his journey, Conall lashed the chariot's shaft together with leather lacings and slowly drove back toward Emain Macha.

"When Cúchulainn got to Loch Echtra, he was disappointed to find no one there. His charioteer hid his grin behind his hand and pretended to be as disappointed as the youth. He sighed and slapped the reins against the horses and shook his head. 'Well.' He sighed. 'I guess there is nothing else for it but to go back to Emain Macha.' He glanced up at the sun. 'If we hurry, we might get back for the drinking.'

" 'No,' said Cúchulainn. He pointed to a blue mountain in the distance. 'What is that peak called?'

" 'Sliab Mondairn,' the charioteer said glumly, realizing that Cúchulainn had no plans for a quick return. 'Most men try to avoid it.'

" 'Take me to it,' Cúchulainn ordered.

"His charioteer whipped up the horses, and they traveled across the dusty plain to the mountain. When they arrived, Cúchulainn looked up and saw a large pile of white stones on top of the mountain. He asked the charioteer what they were.

" 'That is where a watch usually stands,' the charioteer answered. 'It is called Finncarn, the White Cairn.'

" 'And the plain below?' Cúchulainn continued, turning to his left.

"'Mag Breg, Breg Plain,' the disgruntled charioteer answered. 'Many battles have been fought there.'

"Cúchulainn carefully turned, numbering the forts and watchtowers between Temhair and Cenannos. He made the charioteer tell him about all the fields and fords and homes and forts that could be seen from their vantage point. At last, he came to the fort of the three sons of Nechta Scéne, who bore the names of Foill the Deceitful, Fannall the Swallow, and Tuachell the Cunning, who were born from the Scéne River mouth. Fer Ulli, the son of Lugaid, was their father and Nechta Scéne their mother. They bore a grudge against the men of Ulster, for members of the Red Branch had killed their father. Cúchulainn knew their names and stories, for he was a bright pupil when the *seanchai* told of battles and glory while the *cruitire* played their harps.

"'Those are the ones who claim to have killed as many Ulstermen as are now living?' Cúchulainn asked. The excitement of battle began to surge through his veins. His hands trembled and the flesh on his inner thighs quivered.

"'They are the ones,' the charioteer said grudgingly. He did not like the way Cúchulainn quivered beside him or the drumming of his fingers upon the chariot rail. Secretly, he tugged at the left rein, causing the off-horse to dance nervously, turning the chariot away from the three sons of Nechta Scéne.

"'Take me to them,' Cúchulainn ordered.

"'Do you think it is wise to be courting danger alone?' Ibar asked. Cúchulainn turned his head, staring at him. His irises seemed to expand, and Ibar felt his will leave him as he fell into their depths.

"'We are not looking for trouble,' Cúchulainn said quietly. 'But neither will we avoid it if it should come toward us. We are of the Red Branch of Ulster, and we will not shame that house by leaving before we have had words, pleasant or otherwise, from them. They have the obligation of hospitality upon them.'

"Ibar reluctantly turned the gate-horse and drove toward the stronghold of the sons of Nechta Scéne. He tried to take the road that would have led past their watchtower and the road upon which they had pledged free travel, but Cúchulainn quietly corrected his direction. He turned the horses to where the bog and river met, south and upstream of the stronghold. They came upon the pillar-stone on which the three sons of Nechta Scéne had hung their spancel-hoop of challenge. Cúchulainn took it from the pillar-stone, read the *ogham,*[3] then curled his arm around his waist and uncoiled and threw the hoop far out into the river, where the swift current could carry it away from the pillar-stone, challenging the three sons to mortal combat.

"The three sons had observed this and started down from their stronghold toward him. Cúchulainn did not wait on them, however; he lay down by the pillar-stone to rest, telling Ibar not to awaken him unless all three came.

" 'If one or two come, do not bother to wake me,' he ordered. 'But if all three come, then you may awaken me. But do so carefully, standing well back,' he cautioned. And Ibar agreed, for he well knew about the *geis* of Cúchulainn governing that he should not be awakened by anyone.

"Ibar watched fearfully and silently cursed Cúchulainn as a rash boy as the three sons neared them. He knew the stories about them, about their bloodletting and the terror they brought upon their foes when the battle-seizure came over them and their weapons became covered with blood red gore. He knew also that they killed not only warriors who challenged them but the charioteers of the warriors as well, adding their heads to those that ran around the parapets of their stronghold. When black clouds gathered over the stronghold, the spirits of the dead heroes spoke from the severed heads in wails that chilled the blood of all.

Nervously, he yoked the chariot, the coupling rings slipping with nerve-racking frequency from nerveless fingers suddenly as clumsy as stone. As the three sons neared, he carefully pulled off the skins and coverings that Cúchulainn had arranged over himself, marveling at the youth calmly sleeping upon the deep, soft grass, oblivious to the threat coming upon him.

" 'Who is it that sleeps at our approach?' the first of the three demanded fiercely as they came up to Ibar.

"He trembled at the battle-stench rolling from them but forced his fear down and away, trying to dismiss Cúchulainn's throwing of the spancel-hoop of challenge into the river as the frivolous action of a vainglorious boy who saw himself as a hero with a man's laurels draped around his shoulders.

" 'Oh, no one,' Ibar said carelessly. 'Just a little boy who has been allowed out in his chariot for the first time today.'

"The three laughed at this. One arrogantly stepped forward and looked at the sleeping Cúchulainn. He turned and sniggered, pointing down at the youth whose face, free of wrinkle and whisker, remained serene and peaceful.

" 'This is not a way for him to become a warrior,' he said, adding carelessly, 'His luck is gone if he remains here.' He laughed and gestured away toward Ulster. 'Take him and leave our lands and do not bring your horses here again to graze our grass.' He grinned at the others. 'It is a good day to be gracious. We owe a life now and then to the gods.'

"Ibar stretched forth his hands, showing the tail of the reins slipping through his fingers. 'I have the reins here,' he said. Then he felt ashamed of his eagerness to be away from the three sons. 'Why should you act this way toward us? Look: the boy sleeps like a boy should. Why should you expect him to be a warrior when no beard sprouts from his chin?'

" 'Because this is a boy different from other boys,' Cúchulainn said, leaping to his feet. 'This is a boy who came to fight!'

"The warrior who stood beside him laughed loudly, the sound of his laughter ringing off the dark, pine-draped hills surrounding the ford. A cloud moved over the sun, changing its glow from gold to blood red, as if Lugh was smiling upon the boy.

" 'This is a barefaced boy who wishes to be a warrior,' the warrior said. He prodded Cúchulainn in the chest with a thick, greasy forefinger. Foul breath wafted over his rotting teeth. 'It will be a pleasure to teach him a few manners.'

"Cúchulainn laughed, but in his laughter could be heard politeness. He leaned back from the cloudy breath and grinned. 'If you are willing, my wishes may make themselves known in the ford. There,' he said, pointing.

"Ibar nudged the young warrior, whispering, 'Be careful with him. He is called Foill because he is very wily in the ways of the warrior. If your first thrust does not kill him, you may spend the rest of the battle thrusting in vain at him.'

" 'I swear by my people's oath that he will not use his tricks to his advantage today,' Cúchulainn said grimly. 'Nor will he use his tricks on any more Ulstermen! When Duaibhseach, Conchobor's broad spear, leaves my hand, he will feel it and my strength and think it to be that of an outlaw!'

"And Cúchulainn unleashed his heavy spear with all his might. Foill tried to dodge, but so swiftly did the spear fly that it had pierced him and broken his back while he was still thinking which of his many warrior tricks to employ against the youth in front of him. Cúchulainn gave a shout of triumph and immediately claimed his trophies, taking Foill's head with a single swordstroke.

"A shout of anger rose from the other two, and the thin one moved swiftly toward Cúchulainn. His face contorted in fury as he banged his sword against his shield. Foul epithets roared toward them.

" 'Be careful as well with this one,' Ibar warned. 'His name is Fannall, and he is light upon the water as if he were a swallow or a swan.'

" 'That trick, too, will not be used upon any Ulstermen after today,' Cúchulainn said. 'You have seen how lightly I walked the pool in Emain Macha.'

"They met in the ford, and Fannall danced lightly upon the water, but he was not as light as Cúchulainn, and the boy killed him easily and took away his trophies, including his head.

"A battle scream rose from the thin lips of the third. He roared down upon Cúchulainn then, a battle-ax swinging in his hand. Grim lights danced from its red-stained edge.

" 'This one,' Ibar said hurriedly, taking heart at the skill of Cúchulainn he had seen displayed that day, 'is called Tuachell and he lives up to his name: he has never been touched by any weapon. He is the cleverest of the bunch.'

" 'Then I will use the *del chliss* on him,' Cúchulainn said. 'That is a wily weapon itself and will red-riddle him before he can attack.'

"And Cúchulainn's weapon split Tuachell in twain, and he died looking at his guts pooled around his feet. Cúchulainn went up to him and cut off his head, taking his weapons as trophies as well. He brought them back and gave them to Ibar to attend.

"Suddenly a scream rent the air behind him from the mother of the three, Nechta Scéne, as she drove toward them. Madness flared from her eyes, her red mouth gaped wide in blood fury. Cúchulainn took the three heads into the chariot with him, saying: 'These heads will remain with me until we reach Emain Macha.'

"Ibar whipped the horses, turning the chariot toward Emain Macha. Cúchulainn laughed and said, 'You promised us the best driving among all the charioteers. I think we'll need it now, with Nechta Scéne chasing us.'

"Ibar looked over his shoulder at the nearing chariot of Nechta Scéne and uncurled the lash over the backs of the horses, not touching them but letting them know the whip was there. They traveled toward Slíab Fúait, and so rapid was their flight across Mag Plain that the horses overtook the wind and birds flying above them. Cúchulainn could unleash a stone from his sling, stunning one and catching him before he hit the ground. Slowly, Nechta Scéne fell farther and farther behind until, at last, she sadly gave up the chase and turned back to care for the bodies of her children, lying bleeding and headless upon the ground.

"When they arrived at Slíab Fuait, Cúchulainn saw a herd of wild deer in front of him and told his charioteer to stop. Ibar quickly brought the horses to bay, speaking softly to them until they stopped their impatient dancing upon the earth.

" 'What kind of cattle are those beasts who seem to dance upon the air?' Cúchulainn asked.

" 'Not cattle, but wild deer,' Ibar said.

" 'How would the Ulstermen like to receive one? Dead or alive?' he asked.

" 'Every one of them has brought home a dead one,' Ibar said. 'That is not so unusual. But a live one, well, that would give them pause for thought. But it is senseless to talk like this: no one can catch them alive.'

" 'I can,' Cúchulainn said, and so simple was his speech that Ibar did not doubt him. 'Use your goad upon the horses and drive them over the bog.'

"Ibar whipped up the horses and drove them until the wheels of the chariot sank deep into the bog and the mire reached near the horses' shoulders. Cúchulainn stepped out of the chariot, treading lightly, and caught the stag nearest him, the most handsome of all. He drove the horses from the bog and calmed the frightened stag before lashing him between the rear shafts of the chariot.

"Next, they saw a flock of swans, and again Cúchulainn asked which would be better, to bring the swans with them to Ulster alive or dead.

" 'Only the most expert take them alive,' Ibar said.

"Immediately, Cúchulainn threw a small stone at the swans and brought down eight of them. He threw a bigger stone and brought down twelve more, using the stunning-shot both times instead of the killing-shot.

" 'All right,' Cúchulainn said with satisfaction. 'Now gather our birds. I would gather them, except if I do, I am afraid that this wild stag will turn upon you and try to free himself.'

" 'But I cannot go,' Ibar said, trying to keep the horses from bolting. 'These horses are so maddened that I will not be able to get past them. The rims of the chariot wheels are too sharp for me to climb over, and the horns of the stag fill the space between the chariot's shaft. I cannot get past him.'

" 'Then step out onto his antlers,' Cúchulainn answered. 'I will fix him with a stare that will frighten him so that he will not move.'

"And this he did. Cúchulainn took the reins from the charioteer's hands and tied them to the chariot rail while Ibar gingerly walked over the deer horns and gathered the birds. Cúchulainn tied the swans to the leather thongs used to tie weapons to the chariot, and in this manner they returned to Emain Macha with the swans fluttering above their heads, a wild stag docilely following behind, and the three heads of Nechta Scéne's sons securely lashed to the rim of the wicker chariot.

" 'A man advances upon us in a chariot!' cried the watch. 'There is such a fever upon him that he will spill the blood of the entire court.'

"Now, you may think that Cúchulainn was showing bad manners when he turned the left side of the chariot toward the city in brazen challenge, but the blood-lust was still upon him and he did not know that they had arrived at Emain Macha.

" 'I swear by the oath of the Red Branch that I will spill the blood of everyone in this court unless someone is sent to fight me!' he yelled. Ibar tried to calm him, but such was the battle-fury that Cúchulainn could not hear his soothing words; he wrenched the reins from the charioteer's fingers and tumbled him from the chariot with a well-aimed kick.

"Conchobor, who had run to the wall at the watch's shout, could see the tremor of battle upon Cúchulainn and the foam of madness around his lips. But he also remembered the youth's shyness when in the presence of women, and he turned to his court, ordering all of the women to strip themselves naked and go out to the young warrior.

At first the women were reluctant to do this, but when they were told the young warrior was Cúchulainn, they eagerly tore their clothes from their bodies, exposing their breasts and the dark triangles of their lust. They raced through the gates, laughing and calling to Cúchulainn with Scandlach, the wife of Conchobor Mac Nessa, she whose body builds strong lust in the most celibate of warriors, leading them, dancing lightly across the grass to Cúchulainn's chariot.

" 'Then come and fight with us!' Scandlach laughed. 'Here are warriors worthy of the spear between your legs to battle you!' She pulled her long hair high over her head, large breasts bubbling, wide hips shaking saucily. Nubile women, maidens and wives, danced around him, red and gold and black beards winking with pleasure at him.

"Immediately, Cúchulainn hid his face from them, and they tore his tunic from him, stripping him when no other had been able to, and when his manhood became apparent, they paused in wonder, mouths slackening with eagerness. The warriors of Emain Macha took advantage of the moment and seized him, plunging him into a vat of cold water to clear the fire of battle-lust from his veins. The water boiled and the vat burst from the sudden heat of the water. The warriors seized him again and thrust him into yet another vat. The water boiled with bubbles the size of the strongest warrior's fist. Again they thrust him into a vat of cold water, and this time the water rose to his temperature but no higher, and the blood-lust left him and he saw where he was and that he was naked. He tried to hide his nakedness against the shouts of laughter and crude invitations as to what to do with the man-sized pole between his legs. The women looked enviously upon him, their loins becoming weak as they considered his seven toes on each foot and seven fingers on each hand, the seven pupils in his royal eyes and seven gems sparkling from each, and four dimples showing deeply in each cheek: blue, purple, green, and yellow. His hair hung behind, bright yellow like the top of a birch tree.

Scandlach hip-swayed her way to him, men wistfully eyeing her naked beauty and envying Conchobor. She gave Cúchulainn a green, hooded cloak threaded with gold to hide his nakedness, with a silver brooch to clip it to his shoulder.

"Then he was taken to Conchobor and took a seat beside Conchobor's knee, signifying his devotion to the king, and he has held this seat ever since.

"Now, I ask you," Fiacha Mac Fir Febe said, "if one who could do this in only his seventh year would find it easy to triumph over our warriors today when he is fully seventeen years old."

And Maeve breathed deeply at his words, envying the women of Emain Macha.

Cúchulainn's Shield

I suspect the following is a fragment from an old tale that exists in another manuscript, for it seems this is the beginning of a story to suggest how Cúchulainn obtained those arms that later became identified solely with him and were not the hand-me-downs (a poor choice of words but explanatory) of Conchobor, who gave him his first weapons, as related in the previous tale.

Now it was that when Cúchulainn came back from his training he desired a shield to be made for him. There was a law among the Red Branch that the carved device upon each shield had to be different from all the others.

It was Mac Enge who used to make the shields for the Red Branch, and it was to him that Cúchulainn went when he returned from Scáthach.[1] He asked Mac Enge to make a shield for him and to put a new device upon it.

Mac Enge shook his head. "That I cannot do," he said regretfully. "All that I was able to do I have already done. You can see them on the shields of the men of Ulster."

Anger came upon Cúchulainn then, and he said, "I have earned the right to a shield and a right to a shield like none other in Ulster."

"That may be," Mac Enge said, "but I no longer am able to make what you want."

"You *will* make a shield for me," Cúchulainn said, "or you will meet me on the field with sword in hand."

"I am under the protection of Conchobor," Mac Enge said desperately.

"I don't care if you *are* under the protection of Conchobor," Cúchulainn said quietly. "Make a shield for me with a new device upon it."

Then he left, and Mac Enge was greatly upset at what had happened. He was wondering what he should do—for he knew that Cúchulainn was the nephew of Conchobor—when he saw a man coming toward him.

The man looked at him shrewdly and said, "I think you have great trouble upon you."

"That I do," Mac Enge said. "Great trouble. I am in danger of being killed unless I make a shield for Cúchulainn."

"Clean up your workshop," the strange man said. "Then spread ashes a foot deep upon the floor and level the ashes clean."

Mac Enge promptly set to work, and when he had finished doing what the man had said, he saw the man coming over the outer wall to him. In one hand he carried a large wooden fork with two prongs on it that he had cut from an oak tree. He put one of the prongs in the ashes and with the other formed the pattern that was to be cut into Cúchulainn's shield.

And so Cúchulainn got the shield that he wanted, and the name it had was Duban, the Black One.

Cúchulainn's Sword

This is a fragment that appears in Rawlinson B. I believe that at one time it may have been a part of the preceding tale.

Now it was that Cúchulainn's sword was to hang by his shield, and a magnificent sword it was.

It was called the Cruaidin Calidcheann, the Hard Hard-headed, and had a hilt of gold with cunning works carved into it and lined with silver. The point of the sword could be bent back to its hilt without breaking and, when released, spring back as straight as it had been before. It could cut a single hair off the head of a man without touching the skin or cut a man cleanly in two and the one half of him would not miss the other half for some time after.

The Making of the Gae Bulga

(This poem was written by an unknown Irish poet.)

How did the gae bulga come to be discovered?
That is not hard to tell. It was recovered
From the distant east where Bolg Mac Buain
Held it by Cúchulainn of Muirthemhne.

It seems two monsters upon the Red Sea
Named Curruid and Coinchenn didn't see
Friendship in their future and fought
A fierce battle. Each sought

To slay the other but Coinchenn slew
Curruid upon the sea's deep blue
Above the deep abyss and the champion
Bolg Mac Buain found upon the strand

The skull of Curruid. It had fled
From the sea after Coinchenn bled
Its owner in that once fierce battle
That rang across the sea, a distant rattle

Of weapons making blood blanch
In the veins of men, once staunch
Warriors who stirred uneasily
Upon hearing the battle on the sea.

Bolg Mac Buain, the renowned
Warrior, defeated many with his honed
Wild spear that he made from the bones
Of the monster he found by the stones

Upon the shore. But the gae bulga he gave
To Mac Iubar, the brave subduer to save
His people and Mac Iubar next consigned
To Lena his own pupil that great find.

Lena gave to Dermeil the spear of hard
Sharp-pointed head that often bled
Enemies dry. And Dermeil gave that
Weapon to his tutoress, Scathach.

Scathach gave it to Aifé, a most
Foolish act for Aifé came to boast
Cúchulainn as her great lover
And she gave the spear to that rover.

This was the fatal spear that came
To Cúchulainn and by him was slain
Aifé's only son who was the Hound's son
As well. That was an evil deed done.

Cúchulainn brought the deadly spear
Into Erin, with all its barbs. There
He slew Connla of the Battle-Shields,
And afterwards Ferdiad was bled

Dry in the great battle by the ford
During Maeve's battle-march that led
To Ferdiad seeking the White Thighs
Maeve promised along with great sighs

Of passion from her daughter
Upon the completion of the slaughter
Of Cúchulainn. So it was for the sake
Of the red-haired nymphomaniac

That Ferdiad violated his great pledge
When he met Cúchulainn upon the sedge
Of Ulster's lands. But Maeve felt no shame
For her deception. She felt no blame.

The Training of Cúchulainn

An abbreviated and slightly different form of this story appears in *The Courting of Emer*. This tale can be found in several manuscripts.

WHEN CÚCHULAINN WAS A FINE lad and had taken arms, he wanted to go out into the world to receive his training.

His training began in Glenn na Luthaige in Munster with Uathan of the Glen, but Cúchulainn quickly learned all that man could teach him and he returned to Ulster to get further training. While he was there, he and two companions, Conall Cernach and Loegaire Buadabach, were offered a chance to go to Alba, where there lived a warrior-woman named Dordmair, daughter of Donall Mildemail the Soldierly.

The three of them promptly launched Conall's ship, the *Engach,* onto the sea and sailed away to Alba, where Dordmair gave them a great welcome. She had their feet washed and a bath prepared for them. They spent the night there, and the next morning the woman asked them why they had come to her.

"We have come to learn warfare and great feats," they replied.

She smiled and stood and demonstrated for them her feats of valor and warfare. These were great secrets that were not to be taught to anyone, but she could see that there was the making of champions among the three, so she had a five-barbed spear brought to her. She stuck the haft of the spear into the ground with the barbs pointing up. Then she leaped into the air and landed on her breast on the point of the spear. But no harm came to her. Not even her clothes were torn by the sharp barbs. She balanced on the point for a while, then challenged Loegaire, Conall, and Cúchulainn to do it.

"Which of us should try it?" they asked.

"Whichever of you is the most noble," she replied.

Now among them, Conall Cernach, son of Amergin, was considered the most noble and boldest, so he went first. But although he was strong and brave and had many times proven that he could throw straight and true and foes ran from him in battle when he sounded his war cry, he could not perform this feat. Loegaire tried it next, but he failed as well.

"It would be a disgrace if no Ulsterman could do this," Cúchulainn said. He stood up, leaped into the air, and hovered above the spear points before landing gently upon them. "It wouldn't bother me if this were my resting place for the rest of the day," he said.

Dordmair looked at the others and said, "You can keep all the honor and awards that you have earned up to now. But now your blood has dried up and your sinews have hardened. From now on, you will gain no honor from feats of heroism. If you wish," she said mockingly, "I can teach you to be servants." But Conall refused for both of them.

Dordmair then asked Cúchulainn to stay with her, and they all agreed that he should. Conall and Loegaire said their good-byes and returned to Erin while Cúchulainn stayed and studied the arts of war.

One day a year later Cúchulainn was practicing the feats he had learned when a huge, solitary man, skin as black as coal, came to him from the shore.

"What are you doing?" the man asked.

"I am practicing what I have learned over the past year," Cúchulainn said.

The man laughed. "Well, they are good feats, there's no doubt about that. But where the feats of heroism are learned, these are not counted among them."

"Is that true?" demanded Cúchulainn.

"It is."

"Is there somewhere in the world where there is a greater warrior-woman than the one I'm with now?" Cúchulainn asked.

"There is," the man said. "Scáthach, daughter of Buan-uinne, king of Scythia, in the far East."

"I've heard of her before," Cúchulainn said respectfully.

"I'm certain that you have. But it's a long way from here to there for such a little man."

Cúchulainn's temper flared for a second, but he swallowed his pride and said, "Will you tell me how to get there?"

The man laughed. "No, why should I?"

"Then," Cúchulainn said hotly, "may your evil come back upon you, you spectral, shriveled phantom! I have come this far without your help. I can go farther."

The big man left, and Cúchulainn took himself to bed. But he did not sleep during the night with the thought of the warrior-woman in the East dancing brightly in his mind.

When the sun came he rose, took his weapons, and turned toward Scythia.

Few people know which roads he took, but he didn't stop until he came to where Scáthach lived. There he saw bright, beautiful youths playing hurley and other games. Without saying a word, he joined in with them, and if one youth was playing well, Cúchulainn would not speak with him until he had taken the ball from him and scored a goal.

At last one of the two leaders of the youths came to him and said, "Why did you score a goal against me?"

"I did it once and I can do it again," said Cúchulainn.

"You never would have if we had seen you at the start of the game."

"You see me now and I'll still score against you."

Three times he scored by himself against all the other youths, and all had to admit that he was the best player there.

Now four men from Erin were there for their training, and they came up to him, embraced him, and asked him for news of Erin. He asked them what feats they had learned in the past year.

"We have to learn the Bridge of Leaps," they replied, shaking their heads and looking grim.

"How long does it take to learn it?" Cúchulainn asked.

"A quarter and a month and a year and three days and three nights."

"Will you show me how to do it?" Cúchulainn asked.

"No!" they replied. "You can learn it from Scáthach like all the rest."

"I'd like to see that," Cúchulainn said.

So they took him to the bridge and showed him that when a man stood on one end of the bridge, it became narrow, sharp, and slippery and rose as high in the air as a tall mast on a ship. Cúchulainn leaped onto it and began to slide down.

Scáthach had been watching the youths from her bedchamber, which had seven doors and seven windows between each door and seven compartments between each window and one hundred fifty girls in each compartment, each wearing a purple-and-blue cloak. There were one hundred fifty boys of the same age, brave champions of great deeds, opposite each door, inside and out, studying acts of war and heroism from Scáthach.

Scáthach's daughter Uathach was with her. She had slender white fingers, black eyebrows, and hair of burnished gold. She was weaving gold thread with a bright-bordered weaver's beam. When she saw Cúchulainn on the bridge, she immediately fell in love with him, and so strong was her love that she could not think straight. Her desire grew, and without thinking she wove with silver thread where once she had woven with gold. She went as white as a lily, then as red as blood, and back again.

Her mother noticed her changing and asked what was the matter. She told Scáthach about the young man on the bridge and how her heart was happy when he finally found a handhold and terrified when he began to slip. She feared that he would never see his mother or father again and that many would grieve for him.

Now Scáthach had the gift of prophecy and shook her head in amusement. "Look well at that youth, for that childlike young man was shown to me not long ago. I saw that he was coming from Erin in the West. I saw that he would find the truth of the Bridge of Leaps in an hour, even though all else need a quarter, a month, a year, three days, and three nights worth of training to do it. I saw that his bold deeds would remain on people's lips until the end of the world and that he would be the Prophesied Son."

At that moment Cúchulainn began to slip and fell back to earth. The three chief scholars of the world cried out, mocking him for his foolishness in trying such a feat without being taught first by Scáthach. Cúchulainn became enraged and leaped up, hovering about the bridge on the wind, and with one mad leap he landed in the center of the bridge. No sooner did his toes touch the wood than he leaped again and landed on the other side.

The three young men from Erin gave a great shout, praising Cúchulainn for this feat.

When Uathach saw what he had done, Scáthach told her to go and fetch him and take him to the House of the Barbers, where he was to sleep. Uathach left gladly and made Cúchulainn welcome on behalf of her mother. She put her hand upon his neck and kissed him, then she led him to his lodging. When they arrived, Uathach told the others there that they were to be good to Cúchulainn, for he was a young boy from Erin.

"Don't be angry with us for what we are going to do to you," one of the youths said after Uathach left. "There are twenty-seven of us, each with twenty-seven spears of smelted iron. We do this to everyone who manages the Bridge of Leaps."

Cúchulainn gave them a long, steady look, then said, "And what is it you are going to do?"

"We'll throw you up onto the ridgepole at the top of the house and throw our spears at you until your body is covered with spear wounds."

"Why?"

"So you will not fear the hardships that are coming," the youth said. "They'll seem like nothing compared to what happens to you tonight."

"I see," Cúchulainn said, scratching his ear. "But there is a problem. You see, I have sworn to allow no man to pierce my body after challenging me unless it's a warrior in open combat."

The youths told him that if he depended upon his own strength only, his oath would not be broken. Then they seized him and hurled him up into the rafters. Everyone started throwing spears and darts at him, but Cúchulainn slowly made his way back down, resting on the point of each spear until he reached the ground.

No one there had been taught that trick. Neither by Scáthach nor Aife, nor Abloch, nor the Queen of the Land of Snow, nor Ess Enchenn. None of them had ever seen it performed until Cúchulainn came.

They seized him by the ankles and threw him up again. This time, however, a great rage seized Cúchulainn, and he grabbed his own weapons and began killing and cutting the youths apart. He cut off all their heads and put them upon the stakes at the gates of the fort so others would see his deeds and fear him. The hundred fifty champions outside Scáthach's door fell to him in the same way.

He stayed in the House of the Barbers that night and in the morning went to the door of Scáthach's bedchamber. He asked if Scáthach was there and demanded that she give him the treasure and jewels that the youths had brought to her.

"Young man, there are far better men in the world to ask for that and more able to get it," Scáthach said.

"None have managed so far," said Cúchulainn. "But I will."

"What? You would fight with me?" Scáthach asked, amused.

"Rise up and see," said Cúchulainn.

"I'll do that," said Scáthach. She gathered herself, but her two sons stopped her.

"No, we will," said Cuar and Cett.

Scáthach tried to stop them, but Cuar, a broad-chested giant of a man, insisted that he would fight Cúchulainn alone. He stood up and came toward Cúchulainn, performing his twenty-seven-feats, his weapons whirling in his hands so that he looked like a bee collecting pollen from white flowers.

Cúchulainn lifted his shield, with its seven bosses around the central boss, adorned with white steel, crystal, and carbuncle, and painted many colors, to his shoulder. He took his heavy-smiting steel sword, hungry for blood, long and sharp enough among a multitude of bronze sickles to cut a hair floating in a stream. On his side was a long scabbard on a beautiful silver belt. He took his two five-barbed spears, with their ample sockets and red hafts and perfectly placed rivets. Then they went to the place of combat and began to fight.

They planted their feet and dealt bold blows. Their spirits were raised, and the echo of the noise they made could be heard in the islands and rough-hewn rocks of the surrounding districts. Cúchulainn patiently allowed Cuar to deal fierce blow after blow until he wore himself out and his legs were trembling and the strength had left his arms.

When Cúchulainn saw this, his strength rose and with one blow he cut off Cuar's arm at the shoulder. A second blow severed his right leg. A third severed his left leg, and he fell face down on top of Cúchulainn. He bit Cúchulainn on the shoulder and tore off a strip of skin from his shoulder down to his fingertips. That was the shearing of Cúchulainn.

Then Cúchulainn beheaded Cuar, son of Scáthach, and brought his head back to Scáthach's bedchamber.

"What is it?" Scáthach asked.

"Do you recognize this head?"

"I do. You have done a violent deed, Cúchulainn. A bed will be made for you at my feet, and a healer will tend your wounds for three months."

That night Uathach came to the room where Cúchulainn was sleeping. He awoke when she entered the room naked, her beautiful body blushing red with the thought of what was to come.

"What brings you here at this hour?" Cúchulainn asked.

"Attack is the best form of defense," she murmured and lay down naked beside him, her breast hard against his side.

But Cúchulainn moved away from her, saying, "Don't you know that it is forbidden for a sick man to sleep with a woman?"

She sighed deeply, then rose and went back to her room and dressed herself. But then she returned to Cúchulainn and lay down beside him again. Cúchulainn was angry at this and reached out his good hand to her. He caught her finger a glancing blow, which tore the skin from her hand and hurt her.

"May your evil come back to you!" cried Uathach. "It's shameful to kill women, you know! You could have just sent me away!"

"I prefer to send you away like this," replied Cúchulainn. "It will disgrace you more."

Uathach pouted and said, "I will forgive you if you don't put me out of your bed tonight."

"You little manx! This is what you wanted all night!" Cúchulainn said. "Go away."

She pouted, then looked at him from beneath half-lowered lids and purred, "If you let me stay with you tonight, I will talk my mother into teaching you the three feats that she has never taught to anyone else—Cuar's feat, Cett's feat, and the feat of eight waters."

Cúchulainn sighed. "I have your word on that."

She nodded eagerly, and Cúchulainn, resigned, gave in and gave her what she wanted. The next day he asked her what the three feats were and how he was to obtain them from her mother. "If Scáthach has never taught them to anyone else," he said, "then it goes without saying that she doesn't want to teach them, for surely worthy warriors have come this way before."

Uathach smiled and stretched and yawned. "I'll tell you how to do it. When Scáthach goes to speak with her gods, she always carries a feat-basket with her. *But* she goes unarmed. If you can find her without her weapons, you will be able to get her to teach you those feats." She smiled seductively and moved closer to him. "But she won't be going to the oak tree beside the Bridge of Leaps until tomorrow. So—"

The next morning Cúchulainn crept up to the Bridge of Leaps and found Scáthach there without her basket. Normally she would have sensed him near her, but she was intent on a vision that had come upon her. She didn't notice him until she saw the light glinting off his sword poised over her shoulder.

A tiny smile crossed her lips. "Well, little hound, what is it that you want with me?"

"To give you death," Cúchulainn said.

Her smile broadened, and Cúchulainn shifted his feet warily, making ready to leap aside if the warrior-woman performed one of her famous feats against him.

"Spare me," she said, but Cúchulainn could hear the mockery in her voice and flushed. "Spare me, and you shall receive the rewards you most want."

A strange feeling came over Cúchulainn that Scáthach wasn't as concerned about her life as she should have been with his great sword as close to her neck as a single hair.

"What rewards would those be?" he asked cautiously.

She shrugged and laughed. "Why, what is it you want?"

"I want the three feats you have never taught to anyone else, your daughter for the nights, and the friendship of your own thighs."

Her eyes widened at this last, for a long time had passed since a man had tried to lay with her, and she felt a strange tingling that was almost foreign to her begin in her stomach beneath the heavy scars that crisscrossed her body.

She gave him her word and taught him the three feats. That night he had the festival of hand and bed with the girl and from then on the friendly and eager thighs of Scáthach, and he stayed with her for a year.

Then he met Aife, a beautiful queen from the other side of the island of Alba, and when Aife saw Cúchulainn, she fell greatly in love with him and said, "It would be wrong for you to leave until you discovered all the feats of bravery."

Cúchulainn raised his eyebrows and studied her carefully, for he had heard about her trickery. "Haven't I already learned them?"

"No," Aife said smugly. "I have three prize-feats of my own, and I would be willing to teach them to you, but they take a full year to learn. If you have them, however, you will surpass all the other warriors in the world."[1]

Cúchulainn mulled Aife's words over. It was true that he wanted the feats of Aife, for his purpose in life was to become the best warrior in Ulster, which meant the world.

But what, he thought, would be added to what he already knew? What again, he thought, would it hurt, for a little bit of knowledge is better than nothing.

And so he stayed with Aife for the year and learned the feats she knew. When it came time for him to leave, Aife was anxious for him to stay and said, "You must not go yet."

Cúchulainn frowned warily, for he knew Aife's trickery and how she could make logic dance and sparkle like sunlight on Manannan's waves, pretty but formless and bodiless.

"Why should I stay?" he asked.

"Because," she said, lowering her eyes, pretending modesty, "I am pregnant and it would not be right for you to leave without knowing what child I will bear."

Cúchulainn nodded thoughtfully and said, "I must go. But I give you this to guide you: If you bear a daughter, then every mother should profit from the daughter. You should give her to the man you find worthy of her. If it's a son"—here he paused for a moment—"raise him well and teach him all the feats of a warrior except that of the *gae bulga*.[2] That I will teach him myself when he comes to Erin."

And he left, and she was sorrowful at his parting but refused to let him see the tears in her eyes or sense the ache in her heart as she watched him hurry down the path leading to the Bridge of Leaps.

When he arrived at the Bridge of Leaps, he saw a hideous hag, tall but ancient, carrying a vessel forged from a fist of smelted iron. She was trying to cross from the other side, but the bridge kept throwing her back. She looked up, saw the young Cúchulainn making ready to enter the bridge, and said crossly, "Leave me the road so I can get past you, Cúchulainn. I need the width of two men's shoulders, for my burden is very heavy and I am too old for dainty prancing."

Cúchulainn looked at the bridge and the path that the old hag had to travel and shook his head. "There's room for only one here. The way is as slender as a hair and as sharp as a thorn, and an eel's tail isn't half as slippery as the smooth rock. The thorn of a thistle couldn't stick to this surface."

The old hag shook a withered fist at him and said furiously, "I will curse you and all your travels if you don't let me have this road!"

Cúchulainn shook his head. "Very well. You may have the road, although you might get your death from it as well."

He took a deep breath, then seized the bridge with both arms and legs, but the hag immediately performed the thunder-feat and seized him roughly, wounding him along the back and legs and arms. But Cúchulainn was ready for her and leaped up in the air, hovering for a moment above her, then dropped down behind the old hag and beheaded her with one stroke. This was the Death of Ess Enchenn, and Cúchulainn did the land and world a good deed with her slaying.

Now at this time, Scáthach was teaching some warriors from Erin who had come to her while Cúchulainn was in Greece.[3] The warriors included Ferdiad and Ferdemain, the sons of Damán; Fróech, son of Fídach; Naisi, son of Usneach; Loch Mór, son of Mofebhais; and Fergus, son of Lua of the Long Mane. Cúchulainn arrived on the day they were making ready to return to Erin, but when they heard the stories of his training, they decided to stay yet another year so they could learn from Cúchulainn as they had learned from Scáthach.

At the end of that year, Cúchulainn, who had been sharing

Scáthach's bed, said, "It is time for me to return to Erin with these warriors."

Scáthach nodded, knowing the future as well as the past and the present, and although she knew she would feel the ache of the emptiness of her bed with the young warrior's absence, she knew she could not change the rolling of the wheel of time.

"You shall not go," she said, "until I bind a covenant of friendship among you so that neither one of you will be set to fighting against the other. The only danger to yourselves is from yourselves. I therefore place these restrictions upon you: if the stronger among you picks a fight with the weaker, the weaker man shall win; and in the same manner, if the weaker man picks a fight with the stronger, the strong shall win. Let none of you break these injunctions, for to do so will bring great grief upon you, greater grief than any man has known."

They pledged solemnly that they would obey the covenants that Scáthach had laid upon them. Then they bade her good-bye, leaving with her the fees for her training.

As they made their way home, they traveled through the lands of the Men of Catt. Cúchulainn called a halt and said, "This is where the Men of Catt live. Their king is Aed the Red. Which one of us will take the kingdom from him without resting for a single night?"

"That is a great feat indeed," Ferdiad said. Then he laughed. "Shall we all have a try for it?"

They went forward, but Cúchulainn made his way to the edge of the sea in search of birds or winged creatures that would carry him to the fortress of Aed the Red so the women and youths would marvel at his skill.

On the beach, however, Cúchulainn found one hundred men and one hundred women standing in the shallows of the water. Among them was a beautiful maiden whose face and form were among the fairest in the world. The men and women were all wailing great cries of lamentation and wringing their hands and beating their breasts in sorrow.

"What is wrong with you?" Cúchulainn said. "The day is fine and the sun is shining and the sea is calm."

The maiden smiled sadly at him. "The Fomorians come every seven years to take a tribute from this land of the firstborn of the king's children. This is my time, for I am the dearest of the king's children."

Cúchulainn nodded thoughtfully. "And how many will be coming to claim this tribute?"

"The three sons of Alatrom of the Fomorians," she answered, naming them: "Dub, Mell, and Dubross."

"Well, then," Cúchulainn said, squatting on his heels and staring out toward the sea, "we'll see what can be done about this."

Soon a large ship approached with a full crew manning its oars. A single warrior, dark, gloomy, and evil-looking, sat in the stern, laughing so loudly that his entrails glowed wetly, redly down his throat. When all the men and women saw this, they fled in terror. Except Cúchulainn.

"What is he laughing at?" Cúchulainn asked the maiden.

She lowered her head so that her fair hair swung forward like a curtain to hide her features. "He thinks it is a grand thing that you should be added to this year's tribute," she said lowly.

"It's a sad man who makes a brag about another he doesn't know," Cúchulainn said.

The big man swaggered ashore and lazily reached out his long, sinewy arm to seize Cúchulainn before he took the royal tribute. Cúchulainn slipped away, and with one smooth movement drew his sword and struck off his head.

His two brothers yelled in rage when they saw this and leaped ashore, coming for Cúchulainn, but he killed them as well, leaving their bodies lying neatly neck to neck. Then he sheathed his sword and left without speaking to the maiden, for he didn't think it would be honorable to speak to one who had been abandoned by her people.

When he caught up with the others, he didn't tell them what he had done. Ferdiad grinned at him and said, "Well, then, where have you been? Lazing about while the rest of us make our way?"

Cúchulainn smiled and shook his head. "We all travel at different times and by different ways," he said.

They came to the gate of the fortress, and Ferdiad used the haft of his sword to knock upon the great wooden beams.

"Who knocks?" demanded the gatekeeper from within.

"A band of warriors from Erin," Ferdiad answered loudly. "We are traveling from the East, where we have completed our training."

The gatekeeper took Ferdiad's message to the king, who was mourning the loss of his daughter. But when he learned that a band of warriors from Erin was waiting without the gate, he shook off his black despair and said, "Let them in."

The gatekeeper opened the gate, and the warriors came in. The king rose and embraced each and made them welcome. At that moment the maiden appeared, and the king was overjoyed to see his daughter's return. But he knew that she would have to go back, for the tribute had to be paid.

"Well, daughter," he said sternly. "What is it that has made you return? Are you sorrowful about those who followed you? Or was it fear?"

"Neither," the maiden said, her full lips curving in a dazzling smile that lit the room. "There was a young warrior who came and stayed with me after all my followers had fled. He killed the three sons of Alatrom to save me. To prove that this is so, you may send someone to bring back the rest of the tribute offering."

The king brightened at this. "These are good tidings," he

cried and sent a servant to bring the rest of the tribute back inside his fortress. He told the women in his fortress to bathe the warriors of Erin in perfumed waters. They eagerly followed his orders, for the Erin warriors were straight of limb and handsome as the light.

It was Aife, Aed the Red's daughter, who happened to be the one to wash Cúchulainn, and when her hand clutched his, she said reverently, "Great is the valor and bravery this hand wove today."

The king frowned. "What's this? What's this?" he asked suspiciously.

Aife smiled and said, "This is the hand of he who killed the three sons of Alatrom and ended the need for our tribute. He is the one who saved me."

The king looked around at the warriors who had recently come to his fortress and said hopefully, "Could this indeed be true? When you arrived, was one of you missing from the others?"

"Cúchulainn wasn't with us at the time," Ferdiad said. He laughed. "He went to the shore to try to find birds that would bring him to the fortress." He looked fondly at his friend. "Always the one for the gesture, eh, Cúchulainn?"

"Cúchulainn?" Aed said. "Would that be the same warrior whose fame has spread from Erin across the entirety of the world?" Cúchulainn felt his cheeks glow red at the praise. "If this is so, why then you must take the royal tribute and the maiden that was a part of it."

Ferdiad laughed again and said, "So. This is where you went when you left us, eh? Why, then, may your evil ways come back upon you, you shriveled phantom! Who among us could hope to gain honor and songs sung about him if he travels with you?"

Cúchulainn ignored his teasing and divided the tribute into three parts: a third for the warriors with whom he traveled, a third for the Men of Catt, who had been so hospitable to them, and a third for the maiden's dowry. That night he held a festival for hand and bed for her.

They stayed a month and a day and knew the greatest of hospitality before they again set their faces toward Erin and home. They landed at Tráig na Folad in Ulster and traveled from there to Emain Macha, where Conchobor Mac Fachtna Fathach lived. Conchobor kept the warriors with him for a full year, paying them great tributes from the province. It is said by many that no king anywhere at that time had as many heroes who were as brave and bold as those in Ulster, the Champions of the Red Branch: Conall Cernach, Fergus Mac Roich, Loegaire Buadabach, Cormac Connlongas Mac Conchobor, and the eight warriors who came to Ireland with Cúchulainn.

When the year ended Conchobor divided the lands among them and posted the heroes along the borders of Ulster and brought them tribute from across the whole of Erin as the result of their great valor in guarding the borders.

And this ends the story of the training of Cúchulainn.

Love Birds: Cú Chulainn's Wooing of Emer

I am a cloth
filled with wind
surrounded by the horizon,
a string strung taut
over the sweet intoxicating
undulations of a woman.
Ah, but isn't it tension
that gives rise to notes
and notes that give rise
to melody and melody
what sets the world
a-spinning?

I see a place,
a sweet resting place
a cool shady valley between
two bright mountains
soft as the tenderest of pillows.
But no one lays his sleepless head there
until blood covers the ground
all the way from the
Ford of Scemen to Banchuin.

It is not what she asks you to do;
she speaks
only in riddles.
Does she even know
what it is she is asking:
the death of her father
the immense slaughter
of her kinsmen,

the making of a coat of nails
that will fit you both.

It is just the Gods' way
of letting you know
that love has consequences
And must be prepared for,
that soon you will leave
the house you have known
all these years and grown up in,
to step bravely into a distance
only birds know, only those
who have spread their wings
whether they have them or no
and sounded their solitary songs
into the ripe silence.

                    Mícheál O'Ciardhi

The Wooing
of Emer

The oldest stories and most ancient traditions have Cúchulainn unmarried, but the stories that appear in the later years of Ancient Irish show the popularity of tales of *tochmarca,* or wooings—romances, if you will—and it is not surprising to discover that eventually we have a story developing concerning the greatest of Ulster heroes, the boy-warrior Cúchulainn, taking a wife.

This story exists in several versions, the oldest having been composed in the early part of the eighth century. The story wanders and, at times, becomes incoherent as themes are introduced from earlier sagas, such as the time Cúchulainn goes to Scáthach, the woman warrior who had a legendary school for the training of heroes. Scáthach was supposedly unbeatable as a warrior, suggesting as well that the true strength of arms lies not with man, who is seen as the traditional champion, but with woman. This also suggests not only the Greek and Roman legends built around the Amazons but the ferocity of the woman, which, when unleashed in certain folktales, allows her to defeat male adversaries. Although it would appear that Cúchulainn, with the suggestion of his divine birth, would naturally be invincible, we note that he has a mortal mother, thereby leaving him a Christ figure, a demigod, if you will, in which the human *can* be harmed although the immortal part would remain unharmed. We think of the figure of Christ on the cross, Odin submitting himself to crucifixion after gaining knowledge by giving up one eye, the sacrifice of Siddhartha, the sacrifices of Enkidu and Gilgamesh but, most important, the story of Prometheus, who brought fire to man in defiance of Zeus. We must remember when reading such stories that the archetypal character-hero and the existential significance of mythology are parts of tradition that transcend reality. Cúchulainn seems to be more Promethean, given that his divine patronage comes from Lugh, who is sometimes referred to as the Celtic Sun God but who was, in reality, much more as is given to us by none other than Lugh himself in *The Tragedy of the Sons of Tuirenn,* when he appears at the court of Nuada and is challenged by the doorkeeper (The Watchman of epic form). Lugh describes himself as a combination of all things: a blacksmith, a sower, a reaper, a maker of all things, a doer of all deeds.

"Question me, Doorkeeper: I am a smith."

The Doorkeeper said, "We already have a smith."

"Question me," Lugh said. "I am a writh."[1]

"We already have a writh."

"Question me: I am a champion."

"We already have a champion."

"Question me: I am a harpist."

"We already have a harpist, Abcán, son of Bicelmos, whom the men of the Three Gods entertained in magic dwellings."

"Question me: I am a warrior."

"We do not need you . . ."

"I am a poet and historian."

"We do not need you . . ."

"I am a wizard."

"We already have sorcerers."

"Question me: I am a leech."

"We already have Dian Cécht as a leech."

"I am a cupbearer."

"We already have cupbearers."

"Question me: I am a metalworker."

"We do not need you. We already have a metalworker, Credne Cerd."

He spoke again, saying, "Ask the king whether he has one man who can do all these things, and if he has, then I will not come into Tara."

And so the Doorkeeper announced the coming of the *Samildánach*, the man of all arts.

This is what Cúchulainn must become—or come as close to as possible: the man of all arts, not only warrior but wooer and philosopher as well. The complete man where man is incomplete. Of course, we must always remember that, despite his predisposed divinity, he is also man and, as all men, subject to man's failings as well as his triumphs.

The prophecy of Scáthach that Cúchulainn encounters (*Verba Scáthaige*) is a foreshadowing of *Táin Bó Cuailngé* (*Cattle Raid of Cooley*)[2] and exists in two versions: Version A, an original version found in four manuscripts: Oxford, Bodleian Library, Rawlinson B 512, of the fourteenth and fifteenth centuries, f. 118 b 2 (R); British Library Egerton 1782, written c. 1517, f. 19 b 1 (E2); Egerton 88, written 1564, f. 11 a 2 (E1); and Royal Irish Academy 23 N 10, compiled 1575, p. 68 (N). The four copies are independent of one another. Version B exists in *Tochmarc Emire*. The version used here is reconstructed.

i.

ONCE THERE LIVED A FAMOUS king of Ulster who made his home at Emain Macha. His name was Conchobor, the son of Fachtna Fathach. Conchobor was a good king who cared much for his subjects, and under his rule the country and people prospered greatly.

Ah, but peace dominated in the country, and when people met their greetings were quiet and pleasant, and the harvests full and herds fat from eating fully upon the rich green grass of the vast pastures, and the sea willingly gave up its harvest to those who would gather it. Power it was that made it so, and the law ensured that all would enjoy it, and at that time Conchobor's good lordship made him well-admired among the men of Erin.

The king's house at the Red Branch was greatly admired for its stateliness and the richness of its adornments. The Red Branch was built after the Tec Midchuarta of Tara. The house had nine rooms from the fire to the wall, and all were separated by bronze partitions that towered thirty feet. The great red yew beams were richly carved, and there was no hard-packed dirt floor here; no, the floor was wood that had been cut and planed and mitered and joined so closely and finely that it appeared as if cut from one large tree. The roof was tight against the rain, thanks to the gray slate tiles that covered the wooden sheeting over the wooden beams.

The finest of the rooms was that of Conchobor in the front of the house, where the ceiling was made of silver held up with bronze pillars. The pillars had been capped with cunningly worked headpieces of gold and studded with carbuncles so closely set that the same light appeared in the room whether it was day or night. Next to the king hung a silver shield from the roof beam of the royal house. Whenever Conchobor de-manded attention from his warriors, he struck the shield with his hazel rod capped with gold, and the solid, clear note brought about the silence of all the Ulstermen.

The twelve chariot-chiefs all had spacious cubicles that rounded upon the king's room reserved for them during ale-feasts, and each cubicle was gaily decorated. But not as splen-didly attired as the valiant warriors who came into the Red Branch Hall, their colors rivaling the rainbow for brilliance.

Grand were the times in that hall! Games and music and great songs passionately sung (aye, yes, and ribald at times when the ale flowed freely), and heroes performed mock battles to show their skills. Poets sang and harpers and players on the *timpán* struck up their music and rhythms, and then the great beams rang with laughter and joy.

Now one day the Ulster warriors were resting in the Great Hall with Conchobor, drinking black ale from the great iron cauldron known as *Iern-Gúal*.[3] So great was it that it was filled a hundred times every evening, for the thirst of the warriors was great, and when the music of the evening was upon them the Iron-Chasm would be drained in a sitting. The chariot-chiefs played on ropes stretched through the middle from one door to the far door of the Great Hall, which measured fifteen feet by nine score. The chariot-chiefs balanced on the ropes while they showed their skills at the spear-feat, the apple-feat, and the sword-edge-feat.

Among the chiefs were Conall Cernach, son of Amergin; Fergus Mac Roich the Too Bold; Loegaire Buadabach the Tri-umphant, son of Connad; Celtchair, son of Uithechar; Dubtach, son of Lugaid; Cúchulainn, son of Sualdam; Scel, son of Barnene, he for whom the Pass of Barnene is named, he who had been the great warder of Emain Macha. He was such a mighty tale-teller that the saying came down "a story of Scel's." But none of the warriors could surpass Cúchulainn in quickness and deftness.

Mugain watched Cúchulainn dance upon the ropes and sighed longingly. "Ah, but I wish I could grip his youthful waist with my thighs!" she exclaimed. "I'll bet he could lead us on a merry jaunt or two!"

The other women around her nodded in agreement. And well they should have, for his dexterity in performing the tricks of the warrior, his nimble leaping that always left him in balance, his great wisdom and the honeyed words that made them tingle and their loins grow wet from longing, his manly beauty and the lovely, almost haunting, look from his eyes made even the wives of the warriors resort to watching for his daily walk around Emain Macha so they could quickly place themselves in his path, dressed to tease in their best finery, which left their fine legs showing and their breasts swelling over their bodices. They would gaze longingly into his kingly eyes with their seven bright jewels—four in the right and three in the left—and wonder about the grip of his seven-fingered hands upon their haunches and the playing of the seven toes on each foot upon their own.

He had many gifts, though, that endeared him to the warriors, who might otherwise have taken offense at his beauty and its influence upon their wives. First, he had the gift of prudence (until his warrior's flame flared), the gift of feats, the gifts of *buanfach*[4] and *fidchell,* the gift of calculating, the gifts of prophecy and discernment, and the gift of beauty. But where one has gifts, one also has faults, for the gods strive to keep men with a sense of their own mortality, so the gods had given him three faults as well: his beard had not grown, and this would bring chiding from youths who did not know of his reputation; he was too daring (often his deeds would cause more mature warriors to look away uneasily and spit as if to say, "There goes the rashness of youth" and "Fate, yes, we'll be having a fine funeral for him one of these days if he should live so long"), and he was too beautiful.

It was this last that disturbed the elder warriors the most, for even the most patient husband gets tired of being held up to comparison with a younger warrior. It was the fine fettle of women that finally brought the men of Ulster into council.

"Something needs doing," growled one grizzled warrior to Fergus Mac Roich. "A man cannot walk across the grounds without stumbling over women and maidens sighing and cooing like pouter pigeons over his passing."

"Do you know how much Cúchulainn is costing me in fine gowns for my wife?" complained another. "Why she claims that they're made for me but it's been a long time passing since I've seen her in them other than marching back and forth on the green with the others, pretending to visit while their eyes move upon his approach."

Fergus belched and spread the fingers of one hand, the other carefully clutching a drinking horn filled with honey ale made from the first gathering of the season. His eyes were bloodshot but sympathetic. He knew the feelings of the others but had no complaints, for seven women it took a night for him to be sated, and it wasn't his own vain bragging that caused the women to compare him to a stallion. "Ah, now, I know 'tis hard to hold your temper when the lad's about the place, but he's only a lad, and time will put a thickening on that waist and a bit of frost in his hair and then we'll see—"

"And wasn't it just the other day that I saw him talking and walking with Nessa, your wife, Fergus?"

Slowly Fergus straightened and stared across the room at the other warrior, who met his eye unflinching. "Perhaps you're right," he said. "Maybe it's time that we do a thing or two about that."

"Aye, but what?" Conall griped. His strong fingers pulled hard at his beard, a habit he had when working himself up into a rage. " 'Tisn't an easy thing to do, and you know the trouble we'll have if one of us takes exception to him."

"And not from him, either," Scel said. "My wife's tongue is twice as sharp as Cúchulainn's sword and will fair flay the hide off me. As will yours," he added, glancing around at the others to include them when chuckles followed his words. "We're all in the same kettle here, and none of you say otherwise, for you know there isn't a woman or maiden at Emain Macha who wouldn't willingly tumble into the hay with him."

But the greatest worry among the great warriors of Ulster was not so much Cúchulainn laying with their wives and daughters and sisters (for he was very discreet about such matters), it was that a great fear had come on them from watching the young warrior's battle tactics and the recklessness with which he pursued his enemies, and him without an heir to carry on if he should (perish the thought!) die young and early.

So to address those two grave matters, Fergus figured out that it would be good for the Red Branch if Cúchulainn had a wife, which would make him less likely to break the maidenheads of their daughters or steal the loves of their wives *and* would give him the opportunity to sire a son, who would be a rebirth of Cúchulainn himself.

When Conchobor was approached with the idea, he embraced it enthusiastically, for he had noticed the wayward eyes of heavy-breasted Mugain and the way the smoke came into her eyes when she laid them upon the warrior-youth. So Conchobor sent nine men into each province of Erin, into every city and hill-fort, visiting the strongholds, the inns, the hostels, visiting with chiefs and kings, for not just any woman would do for Cúchulainn. No, she would have to be a special woman, as quick-witted as himself, honorable, and lusty to match the youth who carried no peg between his legs.

Yet all the messengers returned that day a year later without the name of a single woman they judged worthy of their young champion to woo. Now word had come to Emain Macha about a young woman at Luglocta Logo[5] called Emer, the daughter of Forgall Monach.[6]

Cúchulainn ordered his charioteer, Laeg Mac Riangabra, to make ready his chariot and the Black of Saingleu and the Gray of Macha. Cúchulainn dressed himself in his best cloak with the gold thread running through it that marked him as royalty, and together they set off for Luglocta Logo. Cúchulainn's horses were so fast that no other team in Erin could keep up with them, and soon they came to the land of Forgall the Trickster.

There Cúchulainn found Emer upon the playing field with her foster sisters, daughters of the landowners who lived around Forgall's land. The women sat in a ring upon the green grass, plying their needles as they worked at learning the art of needlework and fine crafts from Emer, whose skill in such things was known far and wide. Of all of Erin's maidens, she was the one that Cúchulainn had decided to woo, for she had six great gifts that endeared her to him: the gift of beauty, the gift of voice, the gift of sweet speech, the gift of needlework, the gift of wisdom, and the gift of chastity, all of which recommended her highly to him, for Cúchulainn had said before that no maiden would go with him who was not his equal in age and form and race, in skill and deftness, the best handiworker of the maidens of Erin. No other would be a fitting wife for him. But here was such a woman, the only one known in Erin to possess all the gifts needed for a man such as Cúchulainn.

Cúchulainn dressed himself in his most festal attire and went forward to talk with her and to show her his great beauty upon the very day he arrived at Forgall's stronghold. The maidens were sitting on the bench of gathering at Forgall's fort when suddenly their quiet talk was broken by the clatter of horses' hooves, the creaking of chariot wickerwork, the rattle of chains and snapping of straps, all the sound of a hero rushing toward them.

"Look and tell us who's coming," Emer said.

Fial, daughter of Forgall, stood at Emer's bidding and stared out across the plain. "I see plainly two steeds, alike in size and beauty, fierce and fast, bounding side by side. Their long manes and tails flow long behind them like Nemain's scarf.[7] On the right side of the chariot pole is a gray horse, broad in the haunches, fierce, swift, and wild. His hooves thunder on the ground as he takes small bounds, his head erect and huge chest thrust out against the world. Beneath his four hard hooves the grass seems to burst into flame. A flock of birds follows them, but as he makes his way along the road, a flash of breath darts from him and a blast of ruddy flaming sparks pours from his jaws.

"On the left side of the chariot pole is a jet black horse with a finely knit head, his hooves broad and legs slender. His mane is long and curly, as is his tail. Heavy curls lay down his broad forehead. He is spirited and seems followed by fire as he leaps along, stamping hard upon the ground. Beautiful he is as he easily outraces the other horses of the land, bounding over the hard sward along the levels of the mid-glen, where nothing stands in his way.

"I see a chariot of fine wood and hard wickerwork moving on white bronze wheels. The shaft is of bright silver and mounted on white bronze. The high frame is of creaking copper that has been rounded and firmed by skilled hands. A strong, curved, golden yoke has two firmly woven yellow reins from it, and the shafts are as hard and straight as the blade of a sword.

"The reins are held by a tall, slender man with curly, bright red hair held off his fine forehead by a circle of bronze. Patens of gold hold his hair to both sides of his head. He wears a shoulder cloak with sleeves opening at the elbows, and he carries a red gold goad with which to guide the horses.

"Ah," she sighed, "but the other man. The most beautiful in all of Erin that I've seen. Dark and sad, wearing a crimson, five-folded cloak fastened around his white chest with a brooch of inlaid gold. It heaves against his broad chest, covered by a shirt with a white hood trimmed in flaming gold. Seven red dragon-gems appear in his eyes, and his cheeks are blue-white and blood red and sparks and fire seem to leap from them. His teeth are a shower of pearls, and his eyebrows as black as a charred beam. His eyes"—she sighed dreamily—"his eyes burn with love. On his thighs rests a golden-hilted sword, and a blood-red spear has been fastened to the copper frame of the chariot. The spear is a curious one, with a sharp, mettlesome blade on a shaft of wood well-fitted to his hand. Over his shoulders he carries a crimson shield with a rim of silver, and upon the shield many golden animals scamper and romp. The man leaps the hero's salmon-leap and does many swift feats upon the chariot. This is no ordinary chariot-chief who is coming to call upon us but a great warrior of the single chariot."

Emer smiled secretly to herself and nodded. "Then we shall soon know who is coming," she said.

"Do you think he will talk to Father?" asked Fial anxiously. She touched her hair unconsciously as she spoke, patting in stray ends that needed no care.

"We will know when we know," Emer said.

At that moment Cúchulainn arrived where the maidens were sitting and wished a blessing upon them. Emer nodded and lifted her beautiful face and said, "May God make smooth the path before you."

Cúchulainn's dimples showed in a smile that sent the girls' hearts to thumping like *bodhrans*.[8] "And may all of you be safe from every harm," he said.

"From where have you come?" asked Emer.

"From Intide Emna," he replied.[9]

"And where did you sleep?" she asked.

"We slept in the house of the herder who tends the cattle of the Plain of Tethra."

"And what food did you have there?"

"The ruin of a chariot was cooked for us," he said.

"Which way did you come?"

"Between the Two Mountains of the Wood."

"And what did you take after that?"

A smile played upon Cúchulainn's lips. He relaxed against the wall of the fort and said: "Ah, then, that's not hard to tell. From the Cover of the Sea, over the Great Secret of the Tuatha De Danann, and the Foam of the Two Steeds of Emain Macha; over the Mórrígu's Garden and the Great Sow's Back; over the Glen of the Great Dam, between the God and His Druid; over the Marrow of the Woman Fedelm, between the Boar and His Dam; over the Washing-Place of the Dea Horses; between the king of Ana and his servant, to Monnchuile of the Four Corners of the World; over Great Crime and the Remnants of the Great Feast; between the Vat and the Little Vat, to the Gardens of Lugh, to the daughters of Tethra's nephew, Forgall, the king of the Fomorians." He took a breath and said, "And what is the story of yourself?"

"Why that is easy," she replied, her eyes twinkling. "Tara of the women, whitest of maidens, the paragon of chastity, a prohibition that is not taken, a watcher that yet sees no one. A modest woman is a dragon, and no one comes near that. The daughter of a king is a flame of hospitality, a road that cannot be entered. I have champions who follow me to guard me from any who would carry me off against their will, without their and Forgall's knowledge of my act."

"And who"—Cúchulainn smiled—"are the champions who follow you?"

"Why that is easy," she said, leaning her head back and meeting his eyes. "Two called Lui, two Luaths; Luath and Lath Goible, son of Tethra; Traith and Trescath, Brion and Bolor; Bas, son of Omnach; eight called Connla; and Conn, son of Forgall. Every one of them has the strength of a hundred and the feats of nine. Hard to tell, however, of the many powers of Forgall himself. He is stronger than any laborer, more learned than any Druid, more clever with words than any poet. It will take more than your fancy tricks if you wish to fight against Forgall. Many have tried, and those tales are in the songs of his manly deeds."

"And you do not number me among those strong men?" Cúchulainn asked.

"If you have performed such deeds and I know about them, why then I would number them."

Cúchulainn laughed, and the birds turned to look at the source of such music. "Well, then, maiden, I swear to you that I shall do those deeds that will be recalled during the telling of the stories about the strength of heroes."

"What *is* your strength?" she asked curiously.

"Quickly told then. When my strength fades, then I fight off twenty. A third of my strength is enough for thirty men, and alone I can fight forty. Under my protection a hundred are safe. Warriors avoid the fords of rivers and battlefields for fear of me. Hosts and whole multitudes and many warriors flee before the terror of my face."

"Hmm," she said, eyeing him curiously. Lights seemed to twinkle in her eyes. "Those are indeed good fights for a youth, but you do not have the strength of a chariot-chief yet."

"True," Cúchulainn said. "But I have been taught well by my foster father Conchobor, who brought me up not as a churl does his children between flag and kneading-trough, the fire and wall, nor on the floor of a single pantry. I was raised among chariot-chiefs and champions, among jesters and Druids, among poets and scholars, among the nobles and landlords of Ulster, so that I would acquire their manners and gifts."

"And who were these famous foster fathers of yours?"

"That is easily told. Fair-speeched Sencha taught me to be strong, wise, swift, and agile. I am prudent with judgment and my memory is sound. When questioned by wise men, I can answer them as an equal and heed their arguments. I oversee the judgments of all the Ulstermen, and because of Sencha's training, my decisions cannot be appealed.

"Blai, the lord of lands, and a relative, taught me the rules of hospitality. I invite the men in Conchobor's province to feast with their king and entertain them for a week, during which time I settle their gifts and spoils and aid them with questions about their honor and fines.

"Fergus is also one of my foster fathers and taught me those skills by which I slay mighty warriors with a courageous heart. I am a fierce fighter and strong in battle, so I guard the borders of the land from foreign foes. The poor find shelter with me, and I am the defender of the wealthy. I give comfort to the wretched and deal out payment to the mischief makers. All of this from Fergus.

"Amergin the poet taught me the cleverness of words, so I could praise a king for his excellent ways and stand up to any man in valor, strength, wisdom, justice, and boldness. I am a match for any chariot-chief and will yield to no one except Conchobor the Battle-Victorious.

"Finnchoem also raised me, which makes Conall Cernach my foster brother. For Deichtine's sake, Cathbad of the gentle face taught me carefully so I know the arts of the Druids and have knowledge of the gods.

"All Ulstermen have taken part in my growth, so that I fight for all their honor. It was Lugh, son of Conn Mac Ethlenn, who called me into being when Deichtine went to the House of the Mighty One of the Brug."[10] He moved his shoulders. "And you? How have you been raised in Lugh's Gardens?"

"Not hard to tell," she said. "I was raised in the ancient virtues, in lawful behavior, to keep chastity, in rank equal to a queen, to hold myself erect in the face of all. I have every virtue that a woman should have."

"Those are good virtues," Cúchulainn said. "So good, in fact, that we should become one, don't you think? Until now, I have never met a woman who could converse equally with me."

"One more question," Emer said. "Do you already have a wife?"[11]

"No, I do not," said Cúchulainn, smiling.

"But I cannot marry before my sister Fial, who is the older. It would not be seemly. And," she said, nodding toward her sister, "as you can see, she is excellent in needlework."

"I can see that," Cúchulainn said. "But I am not in love with her, and I will not accept a woman for a wife who has known a man before me. I understand that she was married before to Cairbre Niafer."

Emer smiled and took a deep breath, her white breasts swelling over the bodice of her dress. Cúchulainn looked at them admiringly. "Fair is this plain," he said. " 'Tis the plain of the noble yoke."

Emer said, "No one will come onto this plain who has not slain as many as a hundred at every ford from the Ford of Scenn Menn at Ollbine to Boyne of Bred where swift Brea breaks the brow of Fedelm."

"Fair is this plain of the noble yoke," Cúchulainn said.

"No one comes to this plain who has not leaped over three walls and killed twenty-seven men with one blow with one of each of my brothers in each group of nine and left my brothers safe from harm and taken them and my foster sister out of Forgall's fort along with my weight in gold."

"Fair is this plain of the noble yoke," he said.

"No one comes to this plain who doesn't go without sleep from the end of summer to the beginning of spring and from that to May Day and from May Day to the beginning of winter."

"I will do everything that you have ordered," Cúchulainn said.

"Then I accept your offer. Yet I have one more question: Who are you?"

"I am the nephew of the man who disappears in another in the Wood of Badb,"[12] he said.

"And your name?"

"I am the hero of the plague that befalls dogs."[13]

And with that Cúchulainn climbed back in his chariot and ordered Laeg to drive him away.

While they were crossing Mag Breg, Laeg asked, "Now what was that all about?" Cúchulainn raised a questioning eyebrow. "You know," Laeg said impatiently. "That silly babble you had with that woman. If you go to court a woman, you need to speak courting language. Tell her how beautiful she is, how you cannot live without her, but that meaningless drivel—" He shook his head. "What sort of game is that to be playing with a woman?"

"It was a courting game," Cúchulainn answered. "That is why we spoke in riddles, so the other women would not understand what we were saying. Forgall would not give his consent to our wedding, you know."

"Yes," Laeg said, frowning. "But what did it mean?"

"She asked, 'Where did you come from?'"

"I said, 'From Intide Emna.' By that I meant Emain Macha, which took its name from Macha, daughter of Aed the Red, one of the three kings of Ireland. When he died, Macha asked for the kingship, but the sons of Dithorba said they would not give the kingship to a woman. She fought them and routed them, and they went in exile to the wild places of Connacht. After time had passed, she went in search of them and took them captive by treachery. She brought them back to Ulster in chains. The men wanted to kill them but she said, 'No, for that will disgrace me and my kingdom. But they will be my servants. Let them dig a fort for me that shall be the seat of Ulster forever.' She took a gold pin from her cloak and marked out the boundaries of the fort for them to follow. That is where its name came: from a brooch of Macha.

"The man in whose house we slept is Ronca, Conchobor's fisherman. I said that he was 'a man that tends cattle,' for he catches fish on his line under the sea, and the fish are the cattle of the sea, and the sea is the Plain of Tethra, a Fomorian king of kings.

" 'Our food was the ruin of a chariot' refers to the foal that was cooked for us on the hearth, for it is the horse that holds up the chariot.

" 'Between the Two Mountains of the Wood' refers to the two mountains between which we passed: Slieve Fuad to the west and Slieve Cuilinn to the east. We were in Oircil between them; that is the name of the forest we passed through.

" 'The road from the Cover of the Sea' is the Plain of Muir-themne. This is how it got its name. Once a magic sea set on it with a sea turtle living in the sea that sucked men down until the Dagda came with his club of anger and sang an enchantment to draw the sea away:

> " 'Let a hard and great silence fall upon your hollow head
> And silence fall again upon your dark body like lead
> And another silence upon your dark brow in your bed.'

" 'Over the Great Secret of the Mean of Dea' is a wonderful secret and a wonderful whisper because that was where the gathering was first whispered by the Tuatha De Danann for the Battle of Mag Tuireadh.

" 'Over the Horses of Emain' refers to the time when Ema Nemed, son of Nama, reigned over the Gaels. He had two horses reared for him in Sídhe Ercman of the Tuatha De Danann, and when those horses were freed from the Sídhe, a bright stream burst from the ground and came after them. The foam spread over the land for a full year. That place was named Uanib.

"When I mentioned 'the Back of the Great Sow' I referred to Drimne Breg, the Ridge of Bregin. It appeared as the shape of a pig to the Miliseans on every hill in Ireland when they came across the sea.

"The next was a bit tricky: When I said: 'The Valley of the Great Dam between the God and his Druid,' I meant, that is, between Aengus of the Sídhe of Bruig na Bóinde and his Druid west of the Brugh. Between them was the wife of the black-smith. That is the way we came: between the hill of the Sídhe of the Brugh where Aengus is and the Sídhe of Bresal the Druid.

" 'Over the Marrow of the Woman' is the Boyne River, takes its name from Boand, the wife of Nechtan, son of Labraid. She went to the hidden well at the bottom of the dun with Nechtan's three cupbearers: Flex, Lex, and Luam. No one came back from that well without being marked unless the three cupbearers went with him. But the queen went out of pride to the well and claimed that nothing could spoil her shape or mark her. She passed lefthandwise around the well—which is a great mockery, as you know. Then three waves rose from the well and broke over her, bruising her two knees and her right hand and one of her eyes. She tried to escape, but wherever she went the waves followed, leaving their names behind: Segain on the dun, the river Segsa from the dun to Mochua's Pool, the hand of the wife of Nechtan and the knee of the wife of Nechtan after that; the Boyne in Meath; Arcait it is from the Finda to the Troma; the Marrow of the Woman from the Troma to the sea.

" 'The Boar and His Dam' is between Cleitech and Fessi. Cleitech is the name for a boar, but it is also the name of a king, the leader of great armies, and Fessi is the name for the great sow of a farmer's house.

" 'The king of Ana and his servant' refers to Cerna, through which we passed, which took its name when Enna Aignech put Cerna, king of Ana, to death on that hill and put his steward to death in the east of that place.

" 'The Washing-Place of the Dea Horses' is the river Ange, for that is where the men of Dea washed their horses when they came from the Battle of Mag Tuireadh.

" 'The Four-Cornered Monncehuile is Muincille where Mann, the farmer, made spells in his great four-cornered chambers underground to keep the plague away from the cattle of Ireland in the time of Bresel Brec, the king of Leinster.

" 'Great Crime' is Ollbine. Ruad Mac Rigdond of Munster was king and had a meeting with foreigners to attend. He set out for the meeting, sailing south of Alban with three ships filled with thirty men each. But the ships were stopped and held from below in the middle of the sea. The men tried to sacrifice to whatever was holding them by throwing jewels and other precious items into the sea, but that did not work. Then they cast lots to see who would go into the sea and find out what was holding them. The lot fell to Ruad. He leaped into the sea, and the waters closed over him. He landed upon a large plain, where nine beautiful women met him and told him that they were holding the ships so that he would come to them. He stayed with them nine days, and they gave him nine golden cups and, during all that time, the ships could not sail away. When he left one of the women said that she would bear him a son and that he would have to return and take his son with him when he came back from the East.

" 'He rejoined his men, and they continued on with their voyage. They stayed away seven years, and when they returned they came by a different route. They landed in a bay, and the sea-women came up to them. The men heard the women playing music in their brazen ship. The women placed a boy on the land where the men waited. The harbor was stony and rocky, and the boy slipped and fell upon one of the rocks and was killed. The women saw this, and they cried out, 'Olbine, Ol-bine!' That means 'Great Crime.' And that is why that place is called Ollbine.

" 'The Remnants of the Great Feast' is Tailne. That is where a great feast was given to Lugh, son of Ethlenn, after the Battle of Mag Tuireadh, for that was his feast of kingship.

" 'In the Gardens of Lugh, to the daughters of Tethra's nephew' refers to Forgall Manach, the sister's son of Tethra, king of the Formorians.

"As to the account of myself that I gave her, there are two rivers in the land of Ross; one is called Conchobor and mixes with the other. I am the nephew of Conchobor. And as a plague comes on dogs, a wild fierceness comes upon me and I am a strong fighter of that plague, for I am wild and fierce in battles. The Wood of Badb is the land of Ross, the Wood of the Mór-rígu, the Battle Crow, the Goddess of Battle.

"And when she said that no man should come to the plain of her breasts until he had killed twenty-seven men with one blow and yet saved one man in nine, she meant that her three brothers, Ibur, Seibur, and Catt, would be guarding her, each with a company of nine. What I must do is strike a blow on each nine, from which eight will die, but no stroke must fall upon any brother. I must carry her and her foster sister with their gold and silver out of Forgall's fort.

" 'Go out from Samhain to Oimell,' she said, and that means that I will fight from Samhain, the end of summer, to Oimell, the beginning of spring, and from the beginning of spring to Beltaine and from that to Bron Trogain. *Oi* is the poetic word for sheep, and Oimell is the time when the sheep come out and are milked. *Suain* is a gentle sound, and it is at Samhain that gentle words are spoken. Beltaine is a time for fire, for the Druids make their fires then with spells, and when cattle are driven between them they are guarded against the plagues for the next year. And Bron Trogain is the beginning of autumn and means the trouble of the earth, for that is when the earth under the fruit goes into labor."

"This riddling game is too much," grumbled Laeg. "It's a straight-spoken woman for me."

And so they rode back to Emain Macha, where they spent the night.

The daughters of the landowners, however, told their parents that they had been visited that day by a handsome young man in a splendid chariot and how he had spoken with Emer in such a way that they couldn't understand the passing of the words between them. When he was finished, he had ridden north across Mag Breg.

The landowners were a bit uncomfortable with this, that a man in a chariot could come upon their daughters and not be challenged by any of Forgall's men, so they went to him and related what their daughters had told them. Forgall recognized the youth from the description they gave.

"Hmm," he said. "So the madman from Emain Macha came here to have a chat with Emer." He glanced over at his daughter and noticed the new blush in her cheeks. "It's obvious that she has fallen in love with him. But this we cannot have. I'll keep them apart."

Forgall the Clever One disguised himself as a foreigner and made his way to Emain Macha, pretending to be an ambassador from the king of the Gauls. He took golden treasures with him as presents along with rich wine, as one would expect from an ambassador. He was made welcome, and for three days they feasted and visited. On the third day, he sent his men away, and on that day Conchobor praised Cúchulainn, Conall Cernach, and Loegaire Buadabach, telling Forgall about their deeds, but especially about those of Cúchulainn, which made the deeds of the others pale in comparison.

Forgall pretended to be awed by what he heard and suggested that Cúchulainn be sent to Donall the Soldierly in

Alba,[14] where he would learn even more skills. After that he should be sent to the famous school of the warrior-woman Scáthach, who could teach him such skills with weapons that he would be greater than any other warrior.

But the real reason Forgall made this suggestion was the hope that Cúchulainn would never return to Emain Macha. He thought that if Cúchulainn became the friend of Scáthach, her wildness and rash bearing in battle would cause the death of the Hound.

When Cúchulainn learned about the school of Scáthach, he agreed instantly to go, as did the other warriors. Forgall promised to do everything in his power to help. Forgall left the next day, and when the warriors rose they made themselves ready and set off on the trip as they had promised.

It is said that Cúchulainn and Loegaire Buadabach and Conchobor and Conall Cernach all left on the trip together, but it was Cúchulainn who first went across Mag Breg to visit Emer before going to the ship to meet the others. She told him that it was her father and not an ambassador who had visited the Red Branch fortress so that they would not wed. She warned him to watch carefully in case Forgall had other plans to destroy him. Both of them promised to remain chaste until they met again, unless one or the other should die.

Then they said their farewells, and Cúchulainn left for Alba.

ii.

Now it was that Cúchulainn and his friends came to Donall in Alba, where he taught them how to heat up a flagstone with a set of leather bellows and dance upon it until the soles of their feet were black or livid. But they were taught other things as well, such as jumping upon a spear and performing on its point. This was called the champion's coil-ring round the points of spears, or dropping on its head.

Cúchulainn took to the training, quickly learning while the others fumbled and mumbled about the daring needed to perform such feats. But Cúchulainn could do nothing to help them, for it was something that one simply had to do if he could or not if he couldn't.

Now this Donall had a daughter named Dornolla,[15] who fell in love with Cúchulainn and worked her best to get close to the young warrior. Most young warriors would have been flattered to have this happen, but Dornolla was an ugly creature, so ugly in fact that if she glanced at a cow the milk would come curdled. She had knees the size of calves' heads; her heels went before her while her toes pointed behind; she had big, dark gray eyes and a face as black as a bowl of jet. Her forehead was as broad as a chariot beam, around which she had twisted her rough, bright red hair.

One night Dornolla caught Cúchulainn in the moonlight. His thoughts were on Emer, so he did not see her before him until he bumped into her and she wrapped her arms around him. "Ah, Cúchulainn! Dearest!" she said, her voice raspy, like a file drawn over steel.

"What's this?" he cried. He pushed her away, then blinked as he recognized her. "Dornolla! What are you up to?"

"I give you my permission to speak to my father," she said, simpering, which only made her ugliness become grotesque.

"Permission? What—" Then Cúchulainn realized what the poor girl was after, and his gorge rose in his throat at the prospect of laying with the likes of her. He swallowed hastily. "There can be none of this now," he said. "There's another to whom I have pledged myself, and she has pledged herself to me."

Dornolla's eyes narrowed. "Another? Before me?"

"One only," Cúchulainn said firmly. "I intend to take only one wife, and that one is waiting for me to return from this trip."

Dornolla drew herself as erect as she could, then spat on the ground between them and said, "Then I curse this night and the day that follows and the others that come after that for you. We're not finished with this yet, Cúchulainn! I give you my heart and you hand it back to me! No, there's more to come of this before it's finished!"

And she left him, storming away into the night, and Cúchulainn shuddered at the thought of having that harridan for a wife. He hurried from the spot, seeking out the others to tell them what had happened and warn them lest they get caught up in Dornolla's rage.

"What? That pitch-faced bitch?" Conall roared when he heard about the episode. "Why, a blind man wouldn't bed that thing!"

"Did she lay a curse directly upon you?" asked Loegaire, the more practical one.

Cúchulainn shook his head. "Only upon the day and the one after."

"Well, then," Loegaire said with relief. " 'Tis a senseless gesture that. One might as well curse the night and the stars for shining as curse the day. Think nothing of it, lad. An empty gesture. That's all it was. Now off to bed, I say. There's been enough foolishness here. Let's put the night behind us."

The next morning Donall came upon the four while they were having their breakfast and sat with them, sharing their bread. He shook his head while he ate and said, "Ah now, I've done all I can do for you, Cúchulainn! You learn quickly and well. But if you want to be better, there's only Scáthach left for you." He pointed with the hand holding the bread to the East. " 'Tis a fair trip to make and a dangerous one. The skills you want to learn must be earned by your passing the journey itself.

That she-warrior takes on nobody who cannot make the crossing. Sort of a test, you see."

So nothing was left but for the four—Cúchulainn, Conchobor, king of Ulster, Conall Cernach, and Loegaire Buadabach—to make the crossing over Alba. But no sooner had their feet touched the other shore than a vision appeared before them.

"What's this?" demanded Conall.

"Home. I think," Loegaire said, his eyes wide and wondering. "But why would it appear to us here?"

Conchobor shook his head. "I think this is a warning to us that we must return to Emain Macha. The Red Branch might need us."

"All stickers and thorns to me," Conall growled. He rubbed his stomach. "My belly's thinking that it would like home cooking too. This fare's all right for a march here and there, but a steady eating of it leaves me aching for familiar eating."

"I'm thinking that the three of us should return to Emain Macha," Conchobor said. "Let Cúchulainn go on alone to that Scáthach woman and bring back what knowledge he can."

"I'm for that," Loegaire said. He turned a shade green. "But I'm thinking that the crossing of that water again and—"

"Have to do it sooner or later," Conall said impatiently. "Might as well be sooner as think about it coming. Get the bad things out of the way so they stop gnawing at you, I always say."

"Is that what you always say?" Cúchulainn grinned. "And I suppose your wife thinks your words came directly from Aengus."[16]

"Now you'll be keeping a civil tongue in your head or I'll knock it out through the back of your throat, I will," Conall said. But nobody there took him seriously.

And so it was that the three left Cúchulainn there by himself to continue the journey to knowledge. They did not know that it was Dornolla who had sent the vision to them in order to separate Cúchulainn from his traveling friends, the better to play mischief with him.[17]

So it was that, alone and of his own free will, Cúchulainn continued on his journey along the unknown road, for the powers of Dornolla were great and she worked her magic against him, bringing evil in a shadow cast over him as his companions departed.

As he made his way, Cúchulainn was sad and gloomy and weary about the loss of his friends and debated if he should continue on to seek out Scáthach or turn back. He had promised everyone that he would not return to Emain Macha until after he reached Scáthach or died trying.

Suddenly he stopped and looked around, bewildered. Everything seemed unfamiliar. He looked behind him but could not remember having crossed that land. He was lost.

He sighed and leaned upon his spear. What else could go wrong? he thought.

A poor choice for thinking that, for scarce were the words out of his mind when a terrible great beast like a lion came toward him. The beast's eyes held steady on Cúchulainn, and every way that Cúchulainn tried to go the beast stood in front of him, blocking him by turning its side to him. Yet the beast did not attack him.

"So what is it you want?" Cúchulainn asked.

The beast rolled its head, staring hard at Cúchulainn.

"Well, 'tis certain that you came for something," Cúchulainn said. "If it was an accident, you'd be on your way by now."

The beast tossed its head, and Cúchulainn had the strangest feeling that the beast was beckoning him. He took a deep breath and leaped lightly upon the beast's back, clutching his sword tightly in case the beast decided to turn on him. But the beast turned toward the East and trotted lightly along the path Cúchulainn would have taken.

Cúchulainn did not try to guide the beast but settled back

and let the beast pick its own way, for he was certain by now that magic was at work, and since he did not know what magic it was, it was better to hold patient to himself until he could see what was coming to him.

For four days Cúchulainn rode the beast's back. At last they came to the limits of the inhabited world, and the beast stopped in front of a lake. In the distance was a small island, and between Cúchulainn and the island boys were rowing a small boat. One of the fellows laughed with delight when he saw the fearsome beast being friendly to a man, since such a beast would have been better suited to making a meal of the man. Cúchulainn leaped off its back and patted it gently upon its head, thanking it for doing him the favor. The beast dropped its head for a moment, then turned and left.

Cúchulainn walked along the shore until he came to a large house in a deep glen. He approached the house carefully, but no dogs attacked him and no one challenged him. He knocked gently upon the door, and a voice called from within for him to enter.

He lifted the latch and stepped across the threshold. In front of him was a beautiful woman dressed in a white gown that covered her from neck to her shapely feet. "Welcome, Cúchulainn," she said. "I have been expecting you."

Cúchulainn's eyebrows drew together as he frowned. "Do I know you?" he said.

She laughed musically, and twin dimples appeared in her cheeks. "Why yes, you do. We were both dear foster children with Wulkin the Saxon. You were learning sweet speech from him while I was there."[18]

"I see," Cúchulainn said.

She smiled and motioned for him to take a seat by a small wooden table. Then she gave him meat and drink, and after he had eaten and drunk his fill, he left and continued on with his journey.

He came next to a brave youth, who welcomed him as well. This was Eochaid Bairche, and after they had visited long enough for the proprieties to be served, Cúchulainn asked if the youth knew the way to Scáthach's stronghold.

"Ah, yes," the youth said. "But first you have to cross the Plain of Ill Luck. Now here you must be very careful indeed, for if you step on the hither side of the plain, your feet will stick fast and you will not be able to move. If you step on the farther half, the grass will rise up against you and hold your feet fast with its blades."

Cúchulainn frowned, studying the plain before him. Then he shook his head. "But I see no path to follow," he said.

The youth smiled and gave him a wheel and an apple. "The wheel will take you across the first half of the plain. Follow its track carefully. Then use the apple and follow its rolling across the other half.

"But," he said, shaking his finger in warning, "once you've crossed the plain you will come to a glen with a single, narrow path through it. The glen is full of monsters that Forgall has sent to destroy you."

"Forgall," Cúchulainn said. "I should have known his hand would be in this at one time or another."

"Yes," the youth said. "But his hand has always been in it, so you could not see his meddling as something new. Now listen carefully: Once you make it through the glen you will come to a deep gorge high in the mountains. You will have to cross this before you can come to the house of Scáthach."

Cúchulainn nodded, and each gave the other his blessing. Before taking his leave, though, the youth told Cúchulainn how to win honor while he was with Scáthach, then told him about the hardships he would suffer in the Cattle Raid of Cooley and what evil and exploits and contests he would earn against the men of Erin.[19]

Cúchulainn diligently followed the youth's instructions,

crossed the Plain of Ill Luck, and made his way through the Perilous Glen to arrive at a camp where Scáthach's pupils stayed.[20]

"Where can I find the she-warrior?" he asked.

One of them grinned and pointed at the island. "On that island," he said. He winked at the others. "But it's a good trick to reach her."

"And how am I to do that?" Cúchulainn asked. "What path do I take?"

"There," the youth said, pointing again, this time at a bridge. "You must take the Bridge of Leaps. But no man can cross it unless he has been fully trained in arms and warfare."

Cúchulainn studied the bridge carefully. It was strangely constructed, being low at both ends and high in the middle. Whenever anyone stood on one end, the other end would leap up and throw him off.

Cúchulainn took a deep breath and tried three times to cross the bridge. Each time the bridge rose against him and threw him off. The others began laughing and making fun of him. "Now why do you suppose a man will continue to punish himself when he knows he ain't going to make good?" one asked the others.

It was then that the *ríastradh,* the warp-spasm, came over Cúchulainn. His hair stood on end, and each hair had a droplet of blood on its tip. One eye bulged out along his cheek, while the other slipped down to the size of a needle eye. He spun around inside his skin, and then the hero-halo came rushing up through him like a fountain of blood and his muscles contorted and bulged. The others drew back in fear when he opened his mouth and gave his warrior's cry.

He made the hero's salmon-leap and landed in the middle of the bridge and, before the other end of the bridge could rise up against him, he gave another leap and landed safely on the ground of the island.

The warp-spasm was still upon him when he made his way up to the door of Scáthach's house and struck the door with his spear haft, driving it halfway through the door. Guards on the other side ran to tell Scáthach[21] what had happened.

"This must be one who has achieved great valor already," she said. She sent her daughter Uathach to discover who had made such an entrance. Uathach had long, slender, white fingers, raven black eyebrows, and hair like burnished gold. For three days she questioned Cúchulainn and upon the third day she told him that if he really had come to study under her mother, then he would have to make the hero's salmon-leap to reach Scáthach where she was teaching her two sons, Cuar and Cet, by the giant yew tree. Once there Cúchulainn should rest the point of his sword between her breasts and not remove it until she promised him three wishes: to teach him without neglecting him in favor of another; to forgo the payment of wedding gifts that he might marry Uathach;[22] and, being able to see the future, she would foretell what he was to expect.

Cúchulainn went to the place where Scáthach was teaching and made his salmon-leap, landing lightly on a basket before her. The startled Scáthach started to draw back, but Cúchulainn had already placed the point of his sword between her breasts, pushing the point gently on the skin above her heart. "Death hangs over you!" he snapped.

Scáthach was not afraid and studied the youth carefully. She nodded. "Very well. Name your demands, then. If you can utter three demands in one breath, I shall grant them."

Cúchulainn named his demands as Uathach had taught him, adding, "And the friendship of your own thighs."

Scáthach's eyes glinted with humor. "Very well," she said. "You will have what you have asked for. And the friendship of my thighs."

That night Uathach was given to him, and the next day

Scáthach began his instruction in arms and gave to him willingly the friendship of her thighs.

Now during the time that Cúchulainn studied with Scáthach and was husband to Uathach, a famous Munster man named Lugaid Mac Nois, a foster brother of Cúchulainn and the grandson of the great Munster king Alamac, traveled east with twelve chariot-chiefs of the High Kings of Munster to court the twelve daughters of Cairbre Niafer. But when they arrived Lugaid discovered that the daughters had already been betrothed.

When Forgall heard about this, he went to Tara and told Lugaid that he was the father of the best maiden in Erin, in both form and chastity, and her handiwork could not be matched by any other maiden. Lugaid allowed as how that pleased him, and Forgall promptly betrothed Emer to him. And so the others would not go away saddened at the prospect of empty beds awaiting their return to Munster, Forgall betrothed twelve daughters of twelve landed men in Breg to the twelve chariot-chiefs who had traveled with Lugaid.

Lugaid went back with Forgall to his fortress for the wedding. But when Emer was brought to sit by Lugaid's side, she took his cheeks between her hands and laid it on the truth of his honor and life that the man she loved was Cúchulainn and it was a terrible thing her father had done out of spite to promise her to Lugaid, knowing of her promise to Cúchulainn. She told Lugaid that if he took her as his wife, his honor would be lost. And then there was the matter of the Hound himself, with whom Lugaid would have to contend, and knowing of Cúchulainn's wrath in battle, Lugaid did not take Emer and returned home alone.

At the same time, Scáthach was warring with other tribes ruled by the princess Aife. The two armies assembled on a plain to fight, but Scáthach had left Cúchulainn behind, bound and sleeping soundly, thanks to a potion she had given him the night before. She was afraid that the young warrior would be harmed in the coming battle, but the potion that knocked most men off their pins for a full day lasted only an hour with Cúchulainn. When he awoke and found that he had been left behind, he became greatly annoyed and went with Scáthach's two sons against the three sons of Ilsuanach, Cuar, Cett, and Cruife, three warriors in Aife's army. But when the warp-spasm came over Cúchulainn, he killed all three by himself.

The next morning the battle was joined again, and the two lines charged into each other. The three sons of Ess Enchenn, Cire, Bire, and Blaicne, three more of Aife's warriors, began to fight against Scáthach's two sons. They started their dance on the path of feats, and Scáthach sighed, for she could see that her sons were outmatched, and then there was Aife to fear as well, for she was known as the hardest warrior-woman in the world. But Cúchulainn sprang forward onto the path, and all three fell to his singing sword.

Then Aife challenged Scáthach to single combat, but the madness was upon Cúchulainn, and he went forward as Scáthach's champion to meet Aife.

"Tell me," Cúchulainn said to Scáthach, "what is it that Aife loves most in the world?"

Scáthach shook her head. "That's easy: her two horses, her chariot, and her charioteer."

Cúchulainn nodded and danced on the path of feats as he went forward to meet Aife. A great thunder sounded when the pair came together, and with a mighty swing Aife shattered Cúchulainn's sword to the hilt. She laughed with a warrior's delight, but Cúchulainn pretended to look behind her and cried out, "Ah, the terror of it all! Your charioteer has just fallen down in the glen and smashed your chariot and killed your two horses!"

Aife whirled to look, and at that moment Cúchulainn leaped upon her, seizing her under her two breasts, threw her over his shoulder onto his back, and raced with her back to the army of Scáthach. There he threw her to the ground, seized her sword from her, and held the naked sword over her throat.

"A life for a life, Cúchulainn!" she said.

"Then you shall give me three things," he said.

"Speak," she answered. "What are your desires?"

"You will give hostages to Scáthach and never fight against her again. You will spend the night with me before your fort, and you will bear me a son."

She pressed her lips together, then nodded. "I promise," she said.

And so it was done. Cúchulainn went with Aife and stayed with her that night, and she told him the next day that she would bear a boy. "I will keep him for seven years, and then I will send him to Erin. But you must give him a name," she said.

Cúchulainn took a gold ring off his finger and told her that she should send the boy to him when he could wear that ring upon his finger. He named the boy Connla and told her that he should not give his name to any man who demanded it and not step aside for any or refuse to fight any who demanded it.

Then Cúchulainn returned to his own people.

As he walked along the road, he met an old woman who was blind in her left eye. She told him to step aside for her. But the road was narrow, and Cúchulainn told her that he could not step anywhere but on the cliff above the sea. She asked him again to leave the road to her. As he could not refuse the request of any woman, he did her asking by clinging to the edge of the cliff with his toes. The old woman passed close to him, then kicked his great toe to throw him off the path. But Cúchulainn gave his hero's salmon-leap, landed on the path behind the woman, and struck off her head. She was Ess Enchenn, the mother of the last three warriors he had killed. She had made herself into an old woman to trick Cúchulainn and destroy him, but she failed.

The warriors returned with Scáthach to her own land, and Aife gave her the hostages she had promised. Cúchulainn stayed there for the day of his recovery.

At last when he had learned all he could from Scáthach—the apple-feat, the thunder-feat, the blade-feat, the supine-feat, the spear-feat, the rope-feat, the body-feat, the cat's-feat, the salmon-feat of a chariot-chief, the throw of the staff, the whirl of a brave chariot-chief, the trick of the *gae bulga,* the wheel-feat, the breath-feat, the hero's whoop, the blow, the counter-blow, running up a lance and righting the body on its point, the scythe-chariot, and the hero's twisting round spear points—a message came to him from Conchobor that he was to return to Erin and he took his leave.

But not before Scáthach spoke her prophecy, chanting through the *imbas forasnai*:[23]

"When you have your champion laurels upon your head
You will discover a great trial waiting for you to tend
And be forced to stand alone against a mighty herd.
Great warriors will come against you and your feats
And their necks will crack from the blows of your fists.
Your sword will strike strokes struck to the rear
And the army will feel Sétanta's gory stream and fear
His hard blade that will hew the conjured trees
And the great slaughter by your manly feats
Will cause many to see the boy-warrior and flee.
Cows will be carried off from your hill and
Your people will forfeit their captives and
Be harried by the armies for a fortnight and
During this time your cattle will walk the passes
While you stand alone to defend those passes
In great hardship against the warrior host.

Scarlet gushes of blood will strike the host
And fall upon many battle-split shields.
A band of parasites that you will care for
Will bring many oxen and people away.
You will suffer the pain of many wounds
Upon you, Cúchulainn, but worst of all
You will suffer a wound of revenge. Gall
Will salt that wound in one of the battles
During the final breach of the army. Cattle
Will be taken but the host will know defeat
From your great red-pronged spear-feats
That will pierce men against the furious wave,
Against the whale readied for great feats,
A whale whose feats are blows from the waves.
Women will wail and beat their breasts
In their troop and Maeve and Ailill will boast of it.
A sickbed awaits you in the face of slaughters
Of great anger and beautiful daughters
Will wail for their great losses.
I see Finnbennach with his hide glossy
Come in great rage against Donn Cuailngé."

It was then that Cúchulainn went onboard the ship that had been sent to him. He was delighted to find friends—Lugaid and Luan, the two sons of Loch; Ferbaeth, Larin, Ferdiad, and Durst, son of Serb—already onboard. They sailed away and came to the house of Ruad, king of the Western Isles, on Samhain-night and discovered Conall Cernach and Loegaire Buadabach there, collecting tribute. From within the house came cries of great lamentation and wailing.

"What is that lamentation?" asked Cúchulainn, frowning.

"It is because Derbforgaill, daughter of Ruad, is being given as tribute to the Fomorians,"[24] a servant told him.

"Where?" he asked.

"On the shore below," the servant answered.

Cúchulainn went down to the strand and came close to the maiden. He asked her why she was there, and she told him everything.

"Where do these men come from?" he asked.

"From that distant island," she answered. "But you should not stand there in plain sight where they can see you."

But Cúchulainn stayed anyway, and when three Fomorians came he was waiting for them.

"What's this?" one said gruffly. "A tadpole?"

And Cúchulainn roared into battle, killing all three but receiving a wound in his wrist from one. The maiden gave him a strip from her dress to wrap around his wound. Then he left without telling her his name.

When the maiden returned to her father's fort and told her father the story, many boasted that they were the one who had slain the Fomorians and saved the king's daughter. But Derbforgaill did not believe them.

It was then that Cúchulainn came to the fort like any other guest along with Conall and Loegaire. The king had a bath prepared for his guests and told his daughter to bathe them. When Cúchulainn came for his bath, she immediately recognized him and told her father who had saved her.

The king was greatly pleased and said to Cúchulainn, "I will give you my daughter and pay a huge dowry for what you have done."

Cúchulainn shook his head. "I am sorry, but this cannot be. But she can come to me in a year, if she wishes. I will be in Erin."[25]

Cúchulainn returned to Emain Macha and told the warriors of the Red Branch the tales of his adventures. After he had rested, he left to collect Emer from Forgall's fort. For a whole year he tried to get in but could not, for Forgall had placed many guards around the fortress to keep Cúchulainn away.

At the end of the year he turned to Laeg and said, "Enough of this nonsense. This is the day that I'm supposed to meet with Ruad's daughter. But we did not pick a place. Let us go to the coast and see if we can find her."

When they came to the shore of Loch Cuan[26] they noticed two birds over the sea. Cúchulainn put a stone in his sling and struck one of the birds. He ran to where it fell, but when he arrived he saw two of the most beautiful women in the world— Derbforgaill, daughter of Ruad, and her handmaiden.

"You have done an evil thing, Cúchulainn," Derbforgaill said. "We came to meet you as we arranged, and now you have hurt me."

Cúchulainn put his mouth to the wound and sucked the stone out, and with it came a clot of blood. He spat the stone and the blood upon the ground and said, "I cannot marry you now, for I have drunk your blood. But I will give you to my friend, Lugaid of the Red Stripes. He is a good man and will take care of you." And so it was done.[27]

Then Cúchulainn returned to Forgall's fort. That was the day that the scythe-chariot[28] was readied for him. Iron scythes stood out from each wheel to slice the legs from enemies.

Cúchulainn made his salmon-leap over the three ramparts of Forgall's fort and landed on the ground inside. Immediately the guard set upon him, but Cúchulainn dealt three blows with eight men falling from each and leaving Seibur, Ibur, and Catt, the three brothers of Emer, unharmed. Forgall saw the terrible fury of Cúchulainn, and fear lanced through him. He leaped upon the ramparts of his fort and jumped down, but he fell wrong, and his neck snapped with a sickening crunch. Cúchulainn did not hesitate. He swept up Emer and her foster sister with their combined weight in gold and silver and leaped back over the three walls.

Cries of rage came from all directions, and Scenn Menn rushed against them, but Cúchulainn killed her at the ford of the river that is now called the Ford of Scenn Menn. They escaped as far as Glondath, where a hundred pursuers came upon them, only to fall to the savage blows of Cúchulainn's sword.

"Great is the deed you have accomplished here," a breathless Emer said.

"Then this shall be called Glondath, the Ford of the Deed, from now on," replied Cúchulainn.[29]

When they reached the hill called Raeban[30] they were set upon again by warriors, and again Cúchulainn slew so many that streams of blood ran down the side of the hill.

"This hill is covered with blood," Emer said. And now it is called Crufoit, Blood Turf.

The pursuers again overtook them at Ath n-Imfuait on the Boyne. Emer stepped down from the scythe-chariot, and Cúchulainn chased them along the banks of the river, his horses' hooves throwing clods of sod high in the air as they galloped north. The clods flew over the ford of the river, and now it is called the Ford of the Two Clods. From the Ford of Scenn Menn at Ollbine to the Boyne of Bred, Cúchulainn killed a hundred warriors, fulfilling the deeds that Emer had demanded. He came away safely from each battle and, with Emer, arrived at Emain Macha shortly before nightfall.

Proudly, Cúchulainn led Emer into the Red Branch to introduce her to the warriors there and to his king, Conchobor. Jealous mutterings were heard from the women, who saw now that the youthful warrior was beyond them, for they could little hope to compete with the beauty of Emer. Several warriors grumbled as well when they saw her, but sharp-tongued Bricriu Mac Carbada smiled evilly and said, "Well, a beauty she is— make no mistake about that! But it won't be you, Cúchulainn, who will enjoy plowing the field between her thighs tonight!"

Cúchulainn's eyes glinted dangerously. "What man here

would dare try to take my place?" he said, placing his hand upon the haft of his great sword.

Bricriu put his hands up hastily, backing away from the red anger he saw glinting in Cúchulainn's eyes. "Now, don't be getting your fur ruffled," he said maliciously. "It won't be a man who enjoys her but the king."

"What's this?" Cúchulainn said.

"Why," Bricriu said slyly, brushing his hand over his beard, "have you forgotten? The first forcing of women in Ulster is always the king's night. It's his right. It's the law that the first night be spent in the king's bed."[31]

A great rage rolled from Cúchulainn at that. The cushion upon which he had been sitting broke, and feathers flew like a snowstorm through the air. He ran outside as Cathbad the Druid shook his head. "Bad. This is bad," he said. "The king cannot refuse to follow the law—but Cúchulainn will surely kill any man who sleeps with his wife."

Conchobor shook his head, glaring at Bricriu, who smiled smugly back, knowing the mischief that he had done. "Someday I hope to see that man come into his own bile," he said. He sighed. "Call Cúchulainn back in. We'll try to find a way around this."

"The law," began Bricriu.

"Don't tell me the law!" snapped Conchobor. "I know the law. And I will interpret it!"

When Cúchulainn entered, Conchobor told him to gather all the herds around Slíab Fúait.

"Why?" Cúchulainn asked, looking from Emer to Conchobor.

"Because it is my command," Conchobor said. "Now do it."

Grinding his teeth so loudly that they sounded like a millstone turning, Cúchulainn left and gathered all the pigs and deer and other animals and birds and drove them onto the green pasture of Emain Macha. By the time he had managed this, his anger had cooled somewhat, and he reentered the Red Branch Hall.

The warriors were arguing hotly among themselves about the fairness of the law when Conchobor held up his hand, silencing the host. "Emer shall sleep in my bed to honor the law," he said. "But there is also the honor of Cúchulainn that must be fulfilled. And to that, Fergus and Cathbad shall sleep on either side of her so that his honor will be held."

The men thought about this awhile. Bricriu started to argue, but Fergus balled his huge fist and bounced it off Bricriu's jaw, silencing the sharp tongue as Bricriu fell senseless to the floor.

The men then told Cúchulainn that all of Ulster would bless him and Emer if he agreed to this. He did, and the next day Conchobor paid Emer's dowry and Cúchulainn was given his honor price.

Cúchulainn then took Emer as his wife, and from that moment on they were never separated until they died.

Riastradh: Cú Chulainn and Emer

Once again, he feels it coming on.
She feels it too but says nothing.
It is something she has learned to live with,
her husband and hero turning
around and around in his skin.
Who but the gods could stop it
once it started? The tiny demons circling
around his head, the dazed, contorted look.
It amazed her that after all these years,
she was the only one who even noticed.
That which saved her, that which gave him
his strength, was now strangling him.
He had conquered all there was to conquer.
Because of him, peace reigned throughout the land,
all its green hills lay quiet and prosperous.
Still, sometimes, he raged. Suddenly and without warning,
the old chant in his chest began its pounding,
but the only enemies he could find were inside him.

Mícheál O'Ciardhi

The Elopement
of Emer

This is a little-known story that appears in the late-fourteenth-century Stowe MS. 992. It is the first time we have a suggestion that Emer had an adulterous affair, despite the many times Cúchulainn appears to have strayed from the marriage bed. Given the story of her jealousy (*The Only Jealousy of Emer*), which is generally considered a part of *The Wasting Sickness of Cúchulainn,* one may reinterpret the common view of Emer as a patient and loving wife who restrains herself from reproach when her husband has an affair.

ONCE, YOU SEE, CÚCHULAINN AND his charioteer Laeg went to hunt birds by the side of Traig Baile, somewhere near the head of Sliab Breag. They left Emer behind to herself in Dundalk.

That was the day that Tuir Glesta, who was the son of the king of Norway, came to Erin. When he arrived at Dundalk,

Emer fell in love with him at first glance. When he left, she and her maid went with him.

Tuir Glesta grew highly arrogant, now that he had Emer, and plundered the Muirthemne Plain and Crich Conaill and the lands of Sualdam Mac Roich. He and his men took their spoils of war to the harbor and sailed away to the Isle of Man, the Isles of the Foreigners, and Anglesey.

When the news reached the ears of Cúchulainn, he and Laeg left immediately for Anglesey, where he challenged Tuir Glesta to single combat. With Emer watching, Tuir Glesta boastfully accepted the challenge, and the battle raged horribly between them.

Cúchulainn killed Tuir Glesta and ransacked his stronghold, burning it to the ground, before he returned home with Emer.

Cú Chulainn and Conlai

Who is this boy
coming at me now
so fierce and full
of thunder, sending
so many brave men before him
to the hills or to Hades?
Doesn't he have
a familiar face,
doesn't his skin
so soft and white
and that reddish brown hair,
remind me of someone
I fought with once
until she loved me?
Strange how struggle
can lead to love and love
to hurt again,
so much rancor
submerged in every
tender moment—
in a long deep life
how many sweet, sweet scars.

Oh, *Aoife, Aoife* . . .
you were the only one
who lay with me
undaunted, and I
the only man
who could
make love to you
and live. What

kind of child
could come from
our bitter union,
from such a madness in the loins,
such fury in the belly,
such a burning in the arms
and legs and tendons,
from a fire so blinding
and so bright
that the only thing to do
is to let oneself be consumed
or to hold one's ground
and take up one's sword
and kill it.

Mícheál O'Ciardhi

The Death of
Aife's Only Son

One would normally expect *The Death of Aife's Only Son* to be titled "The Death of Cúchulainn's Only Son," because Cúchulainn is the principal player in this work, an Irish Sohrab and Rustum story that is, compared with the others, not as old as one might expect. The title, however, is distinctly Irish and reflects an older, matrilinear system of descent that is reflected in the name of the Red Branch king, Conchobor Mac Nessa—Conchobor, the son of Nessa, his mother.

We are a bit bewildered by the fact that Cúchulainn has a son at all, since Cúchulainn is a mere youth when Conchobor sends him away to study with Scáthach. He is a mere youth at that time—if one remembers that he was reportedly only seventeen at the time of the great cattle raid.

While studying with Scáthach, Cúchulainn defeats her rival, Aife, and has an affair with her. He leaves before the birth of his son, Connla, but instructs Aife that when their son has grown old enough to wear Cúchulainn's golden ring, the youth should be sent to him. But Cúchulainn also lays a *geis* upon the son never to reveal his name if someone asks for it. The giving of one's name was apparently an ancient formality. One who asked another's name in certain circumstances was, in effect, issuing a challenge. To voluntarily surrender one's name at a time like this would be to admit cowardice.

Connla grows to a stalwart youth and is thoroughly trained in the arts of war, becoming a mirror copy of his father in everything save the use of Cúchulainn's fabled spear, the *gae bulga,* a terrible weapon that never misses its mark and always leaves its victim dead.

We find a complete lack of emotional restraint at the end of this story, which is not Celtic in structure but appears to have a Romish element incorporated by a late tale-teller or scribe. This story became popular in the twentieth century as the source for William Butler Yeats's play *On Baile's Strand.*

AFTER IT BECAME EVIDENT THAT Cúchulainn had the promise of a champion, Conchobor, the king of Ulster and the Red Branch, decided that Cúchulainn should receive schooling in the use of weaponry beyond that of Fergus Mac Roich. So one fine day Conchobor ordered Cúchulainn to travel to Alba and attend the school run by Scáthach nÚanain, the daughter of Airdgeme, whose skill with weapons had become legendary in her own lifetime.

After many weary days and much trouble, Cúchulainn finally arrived at Scáthach's school and, after many weeks of study and the mastering of many feats, he defeated Scáthach's rival, and Aife, the daughter of Airdgeme, went to him as his lover. When she left she was pregnant with Cúchulainn's son, and the boy-warrior gave her a golden thumb-ring and the instructions to send his son to him when he could wear the ring.

"You must keep this ring for him," Cúchulainn told her sternly, "and when the boy can wear it, send him to me in Ériu." He raised a cautioning finger, but Aife knew it was a command that she dare not disobey. "Let him turn from his path for no one, let him tell no one his name, and let him not refuse battle when challenged."

Now Aife followed Cúchulainn's instructions to the letter, for a great bitterness came upon her when she realized that the boy-warrior was not to be her husband. With relish she raised Connla (for that was the name given to the boy) with the skills she had learned from Scáthach. When the boy reached seven years of age, she gave him the ring and told him where he could find his father.

Connla made his way to the sea, where he found a bronze boat with golden oars waiting for him. He stepped aboard and sat, studying the oars. They were huge and more than a handful for the strongest of warriors, but when the youth took them in his hands, they seemed to change and mold themselves to him. He pulled strongly against the seawater, and the bronze boat shot out upon the rolling waves as a stone from a sling.

He made his way to where the Red Branch had assembled at Trácht Éise for an outing.

"What's this?" asked Condere, son of Echu.

The others turned and found him frowning toward the sea, where the boat bobbed up and down on the gentle sea-swell. Now Connla had a pile of stones in the bottom of the boat, and these he placed in his sling and dealt stunning blows to the birds flying erratically overhead so that the flying fowl fell unconscious into the sea. He retrieved them and blew gently into their beaks until they blinked awake, at which point he released them back into the air. And so he performed the stunning-stone-feat until he became bored. Then he performed the jaw-feat with his hands until his upper jaw reached his eye. As the Red Branch watched, the youth sang, his voice rising and falling

until the right timbre was reached and the birds fell again from
the air and he revived them a second time.

"Hmm," Conchobor said, eyeing the boy narrowly. "I feel
danger for the land to which that boy is bound. If a mere boy
is like that stripling, imagine what the men of his land must be
like—warriors of such magnitude that they would certainly
pound us to dust as a grinding stone does a measure of grain."

"What do you propose?" asked Cathbad, his Druid.

Conchobor tugged at his lower lip, then sneezed as a breeze
of salt air came tickling his nose. His eyes watered, and he
wiped at them irritably with the edge of his crimson cloak. "I
think we will have to send someone to greet him."

"To challenge him, you mean," Cathbad said with irony.
"You warriors think with your swords when proprieties might
be better served. Well"—he sighed—"who is it you'll be sending to meet him?"

"Who but Condere?" answered Conchobor. The man
stepped forward, smiling with satisfaction. "Bid the youth not
to enter this country."

"And if he refuses?" Condere asked, fondling the haft of
his sword.

"A silly question," Cathbad said. "You know what the king
meant. And if you didn't, you should be handing your arms
back to the Red Branch and take up *fidchell* in the sun with
other antiques."

"I'll scatter his ribs from here to Emain Macha," Condere
said with relish.

"Why should Condere draw this duty?" the others complained.

Conchobor laughed. "Why, that's not difficult to answer!
Who else here possesses the good sense and eloquence that may
be required when he encounters the youth?"

Grins came from the bushy beards of the other warriors,
for although Condere could tell a good story with the rest of

them, original banter was not among his arsenal of words and wit.

"I will meet the lad," Condere said, stung by the bold eyes thrown his way. He climbed into his chariot and whipped the horses down to the shore, where the youth stepped from his boat.

"That's about far enough, little boy, until you tell us where you are from and the name of your family," Condere said.

The boy appraised him coolly, and Condere felt a faint dread of recognition in the youth's gaze, but he could not answer to the familiarity that gnawed at him.

"No," the boy said politely. "I will not give my name over to any man or turn aside for him."

Condere shook his head. "Well then, if that is the measure of it, you will not go farther until you name yourself," he said.

A faint smile touched the boy's lips. "I go where I wish and will continue the journey I have begun."

The boy turned away from Condere, but the grizzled warrior had been stung by his refusal—though given politely—and, unused to beardless youths defying him, he said hotly, "Turn to me, boy! You may be capable of great deeds of battle and have good blood running through your veins, but you go too far. The pride of Ulster warriors seems to cling to you, and Conchobor is willing to welcome you. But do not turn your jaws and spears and the left side of your chariot toward me or any other warrior or else you will draw the wrath of the Red Branch down upon you for the insult.

"Now be a good lad, and come with me to Conchobor, who invites you to us. You'll pay an ear, though, if you turn toward me. Now give up this foolishness and come to Conchobor, the impetuous son of Nessa and Sencha, Ailill's victorious son. Cethernd of the Red Sword Edge is up there as well, along with the son of Findtan, whose battle-fire wounds battalions who oppose him. Amergin the poet is there to sing great songs to you as well as the greatest of hosts, Cúscraid." Condere took a deep breath and beamed disarmingly at the youth. "Conall Cernach asks that you come to hear stories and songs and the laughter of war heroes, and Blai Briugu would be greatly hurt if you passed him without saying a word or two, he being a hero and worthy of a greeting from anyone." He shook his head. "It would not be right to shame so many for the sake of a minor point of pride. Now I, Condere, have come to meet the lad who keeps champions waiting on him instead of going to them. I came to meet this lad though he is beardless and doubtless is missing manly hair as well, and I am willing to welcome him *if* he is not impolite to the Ulster warriors."

The boy eyed him carefully for a moment, then smiled. His teeth shone brilliantly in the sun like pearls fresh from the sea. "It is good that you have come, and now we will talk as you requested. As you can see, I have lowered my voice and stopped my unerring cast from my chariot. I have"—he turned to gesture—"collected a beautiful flight of birds with my far-flying little spears and not," he added modestly, "by using the hero's salmon-leap. I have taken a vow that I shall perform great feats of arms against any who oppose me. Go now, and ask the Red Branch if they wish to come against me one by one or together." He smiled and shook his head at Condere. "You may return to them now, for even if you possessed the strength of a hundred within your arms you would not be worthy to fight me."

"Worthy!" Condere nearly spat the word. "Why, you little dog turd! I? Not worthy? Well then, so be it! I shall let someone more worthy come to talk to you."

Angrily he turned his chariot and rode roughly back to the others and repeated the conversation to them. " 'Tis obvious that yon young one has grand ideas of his value and worth,"

Conall Cernach growled at this, saying, "The Ulstermen won't be shamed by a waif while I'm alive." He climbed into his chariot and rode down to the strand to where the young boy waited patiently.

"Delightful game you're trying to play, little boy, but you shouldn't try such games with men at arms," he said.

"The game won't be any less with you in it or out of it," the boy said, placing a stone in his sling. With a flick of his wrist, he delivered a stunning blow that struck Conall in the middle of his forehead with a thunder and shock that knocked him ass over heels, leaving him blinking in wonder on the ground. Before he could do anything, the youth had stepped from his chariot and taken the strap from his shield.

Conall rose, shaking his head to clear the cobwebs from it, and stumbled back into his chariot. He drove back to the grinning host waiting for his return, seeing double from beneath a lump the size of a hawk's egg on his forehead. "Someone else gets the chance to meet him now," he said.

But the rest of the Red Branch had seen the ease with which the youth had dispatched Conall and contented themselves with smiling superiorly while keeping a tight rein upon the iron jaws of their horses.

Cúchalainn, however, was approaching the boy while playing with the arm of Emer, the daughter of Forgall, which she had clasped around his neck. Emer glanced at the boy, frowned, then looked again. For a moment she thought she saw Cúchulainn as Sétanta the boy, before he had earned his warrior name. "I do not think you should go down there," she said.

Cúchulainn chucked her under the chin teasingly with a forefinger and winked, but she shook the intimacies away.

"That is your son down there," she said. His eyes widened, and he turned to stare narrowly at the youth waiting calmly by the sea. "Yes," Emer said. "I am certain of it. He is your son. Do not go down and slaughter your son for the sake of honor. He is impetuous, as are most boys at that age, but one can easily see how well-bred he is. It is not right or fair to take arms against your son, who has performed great deeds. It is time that you remember Scáthach's warning and turn away from the skin-torment of the sapling of your tree. If Connla had kept the left board against you, then there would be a fierce combat. But—Look at me!" Cúchulainn wrenched his eyes away from the lad and looked with amusement at Emer. "Listen to me! I give you good advice. Let Cúchulainn listen. If that is the only son of Aife, then that is Connla and—"

But Cúchulainn had heard enough. "Silence!" he ordered. "I do not need a woman's advice about deeds of shining splendor. Those deeds are not accomplished with the help of any woman. Let the deeds speak for themselves.

> "The eyes of a great king must be sated
> With a mist of blood upon my skin taken
> From the body of Connla fated
> To feel beautiful spears forsaking
> The fair javelin's mating."

He laughed merrily, his eyes dancing with delight at the coming battle. "Whatever is down there, my lady, I would not deny for the sake of Ulster."

With that, Cúchulainn rode his famous chariot down to the shore where the boy waited for him. He watched silently as the Great Hound pulled up beside him.

Cúchulainn glanced at the boy and smiled. "You've done well, boy, with your little games," he said.

The boy shrugged. "Unfortunately, you will not play the same game," he said. "No two of you will come to meet me unless I give my name. Is this the way of fighting men in Ulster?"

Cúchulainn felt the sting of the boy's words and said, "What's this? Must I have a little boy stand in front of me with brave and foolish words on his lips? You'll die, boy, unless you give your name."

The boy shrugged. "That's to be proven with a man's arms."

He rose against Cúchulainn then, and Cúchulainn leaned back and away from the first slash of the boy's sword, narrowly missing the return stroke, which he parried with his own blade. But a mocking smile still clung to Cúchulainn's lips until the boy feinted, drawing a slight opening in Cúchulainn's guard, then quickly performed the hair-cutting-feat with his sword. Cúchulainn barely felt the whisper of the blade over his head, but then anger came within him as his locks fell from his head around his shoulders, leaving him as bald as an egg.

A titter of laughter came down from the Red Branch gathered on the hill above them. Cúchullain smiled grimly and said, "Enough of this mockery, boy. Let us wrestle."

The boy laughed. "I cannot reach your belt, but if I stand upon two pillars, I will be your match."

So he took a position upon two pillars, a foot on each, and when Cúchulainn came up to him, the youth seized him and three times threw Cúchulainn down to the ground between the pillars. Each time his feet remained anchored to the stone and sank into the stone up to his ankles.

They left then to wrestle in the water, and there the youth dunked Cúchulainn twice, angering Cúchulainn, who was not used to such disrespect from a mere stripling. When he came out of the water a second time, he seized the *gae bulga,* the marvelous spear given him by Scáthach and its use taught only to him. He threw it at the boy, and the boy's guts were ripped from him and fell at his feet.

"Ah!" the boy cried. "That, Scáthach or Aife did not teach me! You have wounded me!"

"Surely," said Cúchulainn. Tenderly he gathered the boy in his arms and carried him up from the waves to the sandy shore, where he showed him to the gathered Ulstermen. "Here," he said thickly, "is my son."

"Ah, now!" they answered shamefully, and looked away.

"True," the boy said weakly. "Had I stayed among you for five years, I would have slain men on all sides, and then you, Conchobor, would have ruled kingdoms as far as Rome." A great shudder came over him, and his eyes began to glaze from the hurt of his wounds. "Now show me these great men who live here and with whom I might have fought and let me say good-bye to them."

One by one the men came forward, and the youth clasped each around the neck. When the last had bent forward for the youth's farewell, Connla turned to his father with tears in his eyes and said his farewell.

Then he died.

Great cries of grief followed his passing. Then his grave and a marker were made for him, and for three days not a calf among all of the cattle of the Ulstermen was left alive in sacrifice for him.

And as for Cúchulainn, a great and fierce rage rose within him, and all those around him backed away in fright from him as he stormed down to the sea and with his great sword furiously attacked the relentless waves of the gray, gray sea.

Cúchulainn and Fedelm

This story appears to be a prelude to the story about the pangs of Ulster (see Appendix C). We note that in *The Cattle Raid of Cooley*, while the Connacht army approached Ulster, Cúchulainn spent the night with Fedelm after having sent his father, Sualdam, to warn the Red Branch. It would appear that this at one time formed a larger part of one *remscéla*, a story that provides background to the *Raid*.

CÚCHULAINN AND HIS CHARIOTEER LAEG Mac Riangabra went to learn about *imbas*[1] at the river Boyne. They had *fidchell* and *buanfach* with them in the chariot, which was full of stones for casting and a spear with a strap attached to it for killing fish. Laeg held the reins of the chariot.

Fedelm Foltchaín[2] and her husband, Elcmaire, came over a small hill on the other side of the Boyne. Elcmaire said to his wife, "Overtake him!"

Fedelm said, "Well, now, let me see whether the man on the bench competes with his companion. Something is strange that these two men have *fidchell* and *buanfach* games with them while hunting birds on every slope."

Then Cúchulainn spied a speckled salmon in the Boyne. Slowly he crept up on it, but Elcmaire stepped from his chariot, went to the bank of the river, and cast a four-sided pillar-stone into the river. Cúchulainn's horses shied from the stone and turned the chariot away from the river, spoiling Cúchulainn's cast.

Elcmaire stood grinning as Cúchulainn came to him, but then Cúchulainn hacked off Elcmaire's thumbs and big toes as punishment.

Fedelm saw this and came to Cúchulainn, but when she saw the rage in his eyes, she promised that she would be his lover for a full year and show herself naked to the men of Ulster before going to him.

She displayed herself naked to the men of Ulster a year and a day after that, and it is this that eventually brought the pangs upon the Red Branch, et cetera.[3]

The Cattle Raid of Regamna

The Cattle Raid of Regamna (Táin Bó Regamnai) is one of the early Irish romances called *remscéla*, or preludes, if you will, to explain the central epic *Táin Bó Cuailngé (The Cattle Raid of Cooley)*. It belongs to a series of stories that focus on a group of sagas called cattle raids (*táin bó*). This title, however, is misleading because only one cow is involved and the word *regamna* is a genitive explained by Thurneysey in *A Grammar of Old Irish: gamna* is the genitive of *gamain,* which can mean either "yearling" or "November." I believe November would be more appropriate, since the word for a yearling calf would be *gamuin,* while *re* indicates a span of time or the time of the full moon, as in the Old Irish phrase *noichtech ré nIuil la Aegyptacdu,* which means "the full moon in the month of July." I believe that the original title refers, therefore, to the cattle raid during the time of the full moon in November.

This story is found in *The Yellow Book of Lecan* (c. 1390) and MS. Egerton 1782, which was completed in 1517. The text, however, has been dated to the ninth century. The events of this story are also related to *The Adventures of Nera* and *The Death of Lóch Mac Mofemis* in *The Cattle Raid of Cooley,* neither of which appears in this book.

ONE NIGHT WHILE CÚCHULAINN LAY sleeping in his room in the east wing of his house Dun Imrith, he was suddenly awakened by a cry out of the north so terrible and fearful to his ears that he fell out of his bed upon the floor like a limp sack.

Leaping to his feet, he rushed outside, naked and with no weapons. He stood shivering in the cold night air while Emer, his wife, brought out his weapons and clothes, cocking his head this way and that, trying to locate from where the sound had come.

At that moment, Laeg, his charioteer, came rattling in Cúchulainn's famed scythe-chariot from Ferta Laig in the north.

"Why have you come this late at night?" asked Cúchulainn.

"Have you no ears, man?" Laeg asked. " 'Twas the terrible cry that echoed across the plain."

"From what direction?" Cúchulainn asked, taking his clothes from Emer and dressing quickly.

"The northwest," replied Laeg. "From down the great road leading to Caill Cuan."

Cúchulainn nodded and took his weapons from Emer, then leaped into the chariot beside Laeg. "Then let us follow the sound," he said grimly. Laeg turned the chariot, and they raced down the road, the hooves of the Gray of Macha and the Black of Saingleu rolling like thunder as they galloped along.

They went as far as Ath da Ferta,[1] and when they arrived there they could hear the rattle of a chariot coming from the loamy district of Culgaire. They halted and waited, and soon they could see it, drawn by a single chestnut horse with but one leg and the pole of the chariot passing through its body so that the peg in front was attached to the halter strap passing across its forehead.

A redheaded woman with red eyebrows[2] stood in the chariot, wearing a crimson cloak that fell between the wheels of the chariot so that it swept magnificently along the ground behind. Running lightly alongside the chariot was a huge man, who also wore a crimson cloak and carried a forked staff of hazelwood,[3] with which he drove a single cow before him.

Cúchulainn blocked the road and glanced at the cow. "She doesn't seem to like being driven along this road by you," he said to the man.

"What does it matter to you?" the woman answered. "She doesn't belong to you or any of your friends."

Cúchulainn smiled thinly. "All of the cows of Ulster belong to me," he said.[4]

"You are setting yourself a great task by meddling in this, Cúchulainn," warned the woman.

Cúchulainn laughed, but there was no humor in his laughter. "Now why is it that the woman addresses me and not the man?"

"You didn't speak to the man," said the woman.

"Oh yes, I did," Cúchulainn said. "But you took it on yourself to answer for him. Who is he?"

"He is Uar-gaeth-sceo Luachar-sceo," she said.

"Impressive," Cúchulainn said calmly, but it was evident that he really didn't think so. "Now, since it appears the raven has taken the man's tongue from him, tell me your name."

This time the man answered, saying, "The woman to whom you speak is called Faebor-begbeoil-ciumdiur-folt-scenbgairit-sceo-uath."

"You speak like a cuckoo, trying to make a fool of me?" Cúchulainn roared. He leaped into the chariot and stood on the woman's shoulders, his spear on the part separating her hair into two red waves that fell down her back.

"Don't be playing your sharp weapons with me!" the woman snapped.

"Then speak your true name," Cúchulainn demanded.

"Step away from me if you would know that," the woman said. "I am a woman satirist,[5] and he is Dáire Mac Fiachna of Cooley.[6] This cow is my reward for a poem I wrote."

"Let me hear your poem," Cúchulainn said.

The woman eyed him scornfully. "Do you think you can threaten it out of me with your weapons?" she said. "Move away."

Warily he stepped a short distance away from her until he was between the two wheels of the chariot and looked at her. "Well?" he demanded.

> "From the dark comes the sigh
> Of one who will cause the slaughter
> Of hundreds who will fall and die
> Upon foreign plains for one daughter.
> Hear the loud and raucous cry
> Of the craven raven who will like the blood
> Of the man and beast and fly
> Away from the mighty armies that flood
> The plains of Ulster and in sorrow
> Will women wail their ululating cries
> As husbands and sons fight on the morrow
> For a red-haired woman's thighs."

Cúchulainn readied himself for another spring into the chariot, but horse, woman, man, and cow all had disappeared. Then he saw the black raven on a dead branch in a dead oak tree near him. The raven's cold eye stared directly at him, and then Cúchulainn knew and laughed in the darkness.

" 'Tis a dangerous woman you are," he said.

"From this day forward this *grellach*[7] shall be known as *dolluid*,"[8] she said, and from that day it has been called Grellach Dolluid.

"If I had known 'twas you we would not have parted in this manner," Cúchulainn said.

"What is done is done and what was done will bring ill fortune upon your shoulders," she said.

Cúchulainn shook his head. "You cannot harm me."

"Certainly I can," she said smugly. "I already guard your deathbed, and I shall guard it from now on. I brought this cow out of the fairy-mound of Cruachan so that she might breed by the bull of Dáire Mac Fiachna, the Donn Cooley. So long as her calf remains a yearling, that will be the span of your life. This shall cause the cattle raid of Cooley."

"And that raid will bring me greater glory," said Cúchulainn.

> "I shall strike down all warriors who come;
> I shall fight all the battles they may choose;
> I shall survive the great cattle raid!
> And of those warriors, I know some
> May survive, a few battles I will choose,
> Despite whatever offerings they try to trade."

"And how do you expect to manage that?" she said. "The time will come when you are hot-pressed in combat with a warrior who is equal to you in every way:

> "As strong,
> As victorious,
> As dexterous,
> As terrible,
> As untiring,

As noble,

As brave,

As great,

As yourself.

"When that day comes, I shall become an eel and throw a loop around your feet in the ford where you fight and the odds will swing in the favor of your enemy."

"I swear by the gods of the Red Branch that I will smash you against a green stone in that same ford and you will never be healed by me if you don't leave me alone."

"I will also become a gray wolf and take the strength from your right hand as far as your left."

"Then you shall taste the steel of my spear until your left or right eye is put out and then you will never be healed by me if you don't leave me alone."

"Then I will become a white, red-eared cow and go into the pond beside the ford where you are in deadly combat with a warrior as skilled in the warrior's trade as yourself. A hundred white and red-eared cows will follow me when I rush into the ford, and the *fir fer*[9] of man will be brought to a test that day and you will lose your head to that warrior."

"I will use my sling and break your left leg with a stone thrown from it and you will never receive any healing help from me if you do not leave me."

The raven disappeared then and flew into the fairy-mound of Cruachan in Connacht, and Cúchulainn returned home.

This, then, is one of the preludes to *The Cattle Raid of Cooley.*

Cúchulainn and Senbecc

This story may be found in the late-fourteenth-century Stowe MS. 992.

version a

Once Cúchulainn and his charioteer Laeg Mac Riangabra were traveling beside the river Boyne.

Cúchulainn was practicing the feat of nine champions by killing the salmon in Linn Féic. Suddenly they saw a little man dressed in purple, sitting in a bronze skiff coming toward them on the Boyne without rowing at all. Cúchulainn reached into the water and took both in his hand, holding them upon his palm. "Well, now, here you are," Cúchulainn said.

"So it would seem," the little man said. "I will give you my cloak and my tunic as a reward for my safety. They are special in that they fit anyone, small or large, who wears them. No one is drowned or burnt as long as he is clad in them. They will not go to rags, and the one who wears them will stay his youth. Besides," he added, smiling, "they take on every color that one would like."

Cúchulainn laughed. "But I have them already."

"Take my shield and my spear, and not battle or combat will come against you and you will never be wounded as long as the shield protects you."

"I already have them," Cúchulainn said. "They are here, in the hollow of my fist."

Senbecc shook his head sadly. " 'Tis hard you are upon me."

Cúchulainn frowned. "What is that thing there?" he asked, pointing at a tiny thing in the boat at the little man's feet.

"Ah, now, that's just a wee *timpán*,"[1] said Senbecc. "Would you be liking me to play it for you?"

"I would like that very much," Cúchulainn said. He wagged his finger at the little man. "But there'll be none of your tricks, now, hear?"

"Would I be doing that to such a fine one as yourself?" Senbecc said innocently.

He picked up the instrument and drew his finger across it. Sad notes hung in the air, and Cúchulainn began lamenting at the wailing-strain coming from the tiny instrument. Then Senbecc played the laughing-strain until Cúchulainn was doubled up with laughter. Finally he played the sleeping-strain, and Cúchulainn yawned and stretched out comfortably on the grassy banks of the Boyne and fell into a deep sleep and slept from one hour to the next.

While Senbecc went home . . .[2]

version 6

Now it was that Senbecc, grandson of Ebrecc, from the *sídhe,* came from the Plain of Segais seeking *imbas* when he encountered Cúchulainn upon the river Boyne. Cúchulainn reached down and captured him and asked him what he was doing. The little man explained that he had come looking for the fruit of the nuts of a fair-bearing hazel tree. There are nine fair-bearing hazels from whose nuts he was able to get *imbas*: the nuts used to drop into the wells from which streams would carry them down into the river Boyne.[3]

Cúchulainn looked a bit skeptical at this, but then Senbecc sang to him some of his wisdom and a song:

> "I am not a lad, I am not a man,
> I am not a child in learning banned.
> The mysteries of all have left me gifted.
> I am Abcán, a sage who is gifted,
> A poet from the Segais whose name
> Is Senbecc, Ebrecc's grandson, the same
> One who is from the *sídhe*
> Seeking wisdom for the *sídhe*.

Then Senbecc offered great rewards to Cúchulainn for letting him go, but Cúchulainn refused his wishes. Senbecc smiled and picked up his harp and played a wailing-strain that made Cúchulainn cry in grief. Then he played a laughing-strain that made Cúchulainn laugh so hard that he became red in the face and came fair to passing out. Finally, Senbecc played a soft sleeping-strain that caused Cúchulainn to slumber.

Then Senbecc made his escape down the river Boyne in a bronze boat.

To Fann in the Otherworld:
The Wasting Sickness of Cú Chulainn

Often I stared,
stood and stared,
in wonder.

The deer and the beaver
and the birds whispered
that I did not exist.
The mountains suddenly
did not know my name.
Everything I once loved, I myself,
could no longer find the words for.

Once I felt you
coming towards me.
What could I do
but stare and wait
in wonder? The shifting fate
of my tumultuous brethren,
the urgent complexities
of our land and dwelling
were like once gigantic flames
grown tiny and faint
without the ability to burn.

Once your invisible breath passed over,
the vastness of your eternal love,
once it touched me and entered
oh, I knew then, that this
hero's heart was but a dandelion,
a small puff of down

that your indescribably
tender lips
had blown and scattered.

Mícheál O'Ciardhi

The Wasting Sickness of Cúchulainn *and* The Only Jealousy of Emer

The Wasting Sickness of Cúchulainn falls into the romance category; the story roughly follows the outline of a monomyth suggested by Joseph Campbell. In addition to Campbell, we also take into account Clara Reeve's comment in 1785 in *The Progress of Romance,* "The novel is a picture of real life and manners, and of the times in which it was written. The Romance in lofty and elevated language, describes what has never happened nor is likely to."

Today the term would seem more applicable to works peopled with extravagant characters in remote or exotic places—such as the Otherworld—where our hero is a part of passionate love and/or mysterious or supernatural experiences. *The Wasting Sickness of Cúchulainn* is relatively free from the more restrictive aspects of realistic verisimilitude, as is *The Only Jealousy of Emer,* yet highly evasive truth, that truth which lies at the center of the human heart, is always present.

These stories are preserved in two manuscripts, one of

which is the *Lebor Na hUidre* (*Book of the Dun Cow*) compiled in the eleventh century, while the other is a fifteenth-century manuscript in the Trinity College Library. Both manuscripts give substantially the same account and are, obviously, taken from the same source. The latter, however, is not simply a copy of the *Lebor Na hUidre* but appears to be more polished syntactically and is, consequently, a more professional rendition.

The eleventh-century manuscript gives *The Yellow Book of Slane* as its authority. Unfortunately, that manuscript has been lost, but from the *Lebor Na hUidre* we can ascertain that the original compiler was working to combine two different forms of the story in the one we have today. The first form appears to be more antiquarian; it relates the cause of Cúchulainn's illness and details the trip of his charioteer, Laeg, into the Otherworld, where he tests the truth of a message sent to Cúchulainn that he can be healed only through the intervention of inhabitants of the Otherworld.

At that point the story departs to relate a rather long passage about how Lugaid Red Stripes came to be the *Ard Rí* and the bull-feast at which the coming of Lugaid is prophesied (similar to the prophesying of Cormac in *Togail Bruidne Da Derga*). Cúchulainn counsels Lugaid upon his election, although according to the time line of the story, Cúchulainn is on his sickbed at the time. This section is obviously intended to splice the two stories together. Unfortunately, it does not serve any purpose in the development of the tale. Indeed, the instructional segment belongs to the group of *tecosca* in which *Tecosca Cormaic* is the best example. In fact, some of the precepts in *Tecosca Lugadic* seem to have been borrowed from *Tecosca Cormaic*. The description of a means of divination in this part is called *tarbfes,* or bull-feast, and seems to have come from *Togail Bruidne Da Derga.*

We have to ask ourselves why Cúchulainn sends Laeg to the Otherworld instead of going himself. This seems entirely out of the ordinary for such a great hero. That Cúchulainn is well enough to undertake the journey is suggested by his admission that he will not go "upon the invitation of a woman." We cannot dismiss the idea that had a man extended the invitation, he would have gone. That Cúchulainn refuses to leave because of a woman suggests that he considers woman unequal to man. Additionally, however, we must recall that while Cúchulainn is helpless in an enchanted sleep, two women come forward from the Otherworld and whip him nearly to death. Cúchulainn might also have been afraid, for he knows by this time that he is dealing with the fairy world, which exists in another dimension and is available to man only through a mystical portal in fairy-mounds.

The "saving" of Cúchulainn differs in each story. The older form has him being cured by the son of a fairy king, while in the more "modern" recension, his wife, Emer, saves him. Laeg's journey to the Otherworld is related in the literary recension with different detail in the newer tale, and it is in this recension that the conclusion is given. Consequently, we have two distinct forms, each problematical, one at the beginning, the other at the end.

A problem also exists with the styles of the stories; they are so different that it is impossible to attribute them to the same author. The older form is simply a compilation, similar to a cataloging of events such as one finds in epic stories. The teller inserts passages that do not develop the story and are conspicuous by their inclusion. There is, however, a certain poetic development in the rhetoric, although it suggests the supernatural. The human interest that one would normally expect in a romance is conspicuously absent.

The more literary form or recension is more humanistic, as is seen in Cúchulainn's comments to and for his wife, and the poetic insertions are of extremely high quality. There is a strophic principle attached to the rhetoric that follows the Greek example of having the messenger relate the story instead of developing facts through a narrative of events. Cúchulainn's modest accounting of his own deeds provides a favorable contrast with the prose account of those deeds. The ending of the story, in which the woman from the Otherworld gives up her lover to her rival, is a technique that is not developed in other European literatures for quite some time.

This translation makes use of both recensions in order to give the reader the most complete story possible. I tried to maintain the temper of the story while staying within a modern syntax. Although I was somewhat reluctant to include Lugaid's election and Cúchulainn's counsel to the new king, I did provide them to give the reader the flavor of the stories of old.

I believe that the various differences between these versions are more than simple transliterations from a single tale but are the results of centuries of bardic tradition, in which additions were made as the tales wended their way from court to court. Thurneysen, in *Sagen aus dem Alten Irland,* suggests that the second description of the Otherworld given by Laeg belongs with the older form through the justification of the allusion to Ethne—a possible allusion to Emer—which does not appear in the more literary form. There is in the older piece a touch of rough humor that suggests the attitude of the Ancient Irish.

We do have one translation direct from the Irish in *Irische Texte,* vol. 1, that makes occasional references to the facsimile of the *Lebor Na hUidre* with some words that have drawn literary question included in a glossary by Windisch, who also provides a suggested meaning. Thurneysen's free translation, however, is incomplete and speculates in places where controversy occurs. In the preface to his analysis of the saga, Thurneysen says:

> It was observed by Windisch that the text in its extant
> form contains repetitions and irreconcilable contra-

dictions, and Zimmer (KZ xxviii 594 ff.) attempted
with some success to separate the two parallel recensions of which it is composed; but he fell into some
errors of detail. For Best has established greater cer-
tainty by his examination of the different hands in
LU (*Ériu* vi 167). There is shown that only pp. 47–50
are written, for the most part, by the original scribe,
while pp. 43–46 are two leaves written and inserted
by the Interpolator (H), which have been substituted
for the old first pages (*Die irische Helden- und Kön-
igsage* 413; ZCP xiv 306).

The following work is made from a transcription of the lost
Yellow Book of Slane by Maelmuiri Mac Ceileachair in *Lebor Na
hUidre* from A.D. 11.

i.

Now EVERY YEAR IT WAS that the Ulstermen would band
together and hold a festival that would bring all the chieftains
together and the smallest farmer from every branch and brawn
and bramble bush in celebration of Samhain, the end of summer. For three days before and three days after, yes, even upon
the very day itself would the men of Ulster drink and eat and
quarrel amongst themselves upon the Plain of Muirthemne.
Much trading and bartering went on among the farmers and
their wives for cattle and sheep and pigs, honey hives, and bolts
of cloth, and many a honey ale was quaffed to seal a bargain.
In some cases, where the bargain turned out to be a bit less
than one or two remembered, violent brawls broke out, and
when the interest came upon the fighters, didn't the young ones
wink at each other and make their way out into the bushes and

the woods for a bit of exploring and dallying amongst themselves?

But such was the force of the festival itself, the splendor
and the pomp, the feasting and boasting, and the great games
of strength and hurley and chariot racing, and mock battle
deeds and the songs of the bards and the stories of the *seanchies,*
that although heads were pounding from the many ale-feasts or
the hard fists and heads of other Ulstermen, there was no danger of the Festival of Samhain disappearing, and that is why to
this day the grand festival is held.

Now so it was that once upon a time when the Ulstermen
held this festival, the main reason for it was to give a chance
for the boasting of great deeds done by the men, each of whom
would wet his throat and stand forth when his turn came about
to give a fair accounting of the combats in which he had become
embroiled and of the great courage and valor he had shown in
the time since the last festival. This wasn't as simple as it sounds,
though. There were certain proprieties that had to be observed
in the telling of the tales, and those began with each man cutting
off the tip of the tongue of a man he had killed, which he then
carried in a leather pouch around his waist. (And if the truth
be told, there were a few who wisely put a few sweet-smelling
pods in their pouches against the heat of the day, which might
bring about a certain "turning of the tongues," which would
gather flies around his waist and destroy the dignity of the man
himself with a certain odor that would gag a pig if the man
had been truly successful during the year.)

But the tongues were gathered (some would include the
tongues of terrible beasts they claimed to have battled with),
and the men would stand forth and publicly declare the fights
they had fought and won, one man fairly against another. And
to ensure that the stories they wove amongst themselves were
the true tellings, they would lay their great swords across their
thighs and if they spoke falsely, why then the swords would

turn upon them and the screams of demons would come from the swords to dishonor the men who had falsely sworn.

To this festival of which we speak now, all the men of Ulster came with a great thirst upon them except for Fergus Mac Roich and Conall Cernach, who were busy with their own doings elsewhere. The men of Ulster were impatient to get the great celebration under way, and many cried out, "Let the festival begin!" and "Hang it! There's always the dragging of feet by one or two that lets the sun climb high in the sky and bake a man's pate enough that his tongue gets furry." "May brambles sting their cockles!" complained another. "I say we begin without them."

"No," said Cúchulainn quietly. "It shall not be held until Conall and Fergus are here to take part in all." He said this because Fergus was his foster father and Conall a comrade-in-arms with whom he had exchanged a promise to avenge each other's death if one should die before the other. And although many glared at the great warrior, they had seen Cúchulainn when the great wrath came over him and no one there wanted to face the monster that grew from the quiet lad's frame.

"Well, now, perhaps they won't be long after all," one said hopefully.

"We can play a few games of *fidchell* while we wait," Sencha said. "And the Druids can sing and the jugglers amuse us with their tricks. That will help us while away the time until Fergus and Conall make their way here. And the festival won't be 'officially' started," he added. He raised an eyebrow at Cúchulainn, and the boy-warrior lifted a shoulder in willingness.

So with a bit of grumbling and mumbling, the men of Ulster settled themselves beneath the shade of oak trees and a few hazels standing around, and brought out their game boards and bent over them, soon losing themselves in the movings and sly maneuverings that each brought to the game.

Meanwhile, a great flock of beautiful birds dropped down

from the bright blue sky and hovered over the lake, their bright plumage holding the colors of rainbows and dyes. When the women saw them, a great longing came upon them to possess those birds and, if not the birds, at least the feathers, which they could wear upon their capes and dresses or weave into the braids of their hair. As the day was hot and the women had little to do to amuse themselves, they fell to boasting about how great their husbands were at bird catching.

"Well, now, I wish that I could have a pair of those birds, one for each of my two shoulders," said Ethne Aitencaithrech, Conchobor's wife.

"We all wish for that," said another.

"And if any of us should have the favor of those birds, it should fall to me to be the first," said Ethne Ingubai, Cúchulainn's wife.[1]

The others looked enviously at her, for not a one of them there didn't envy her the nights they imagined she had in Cúchulainn's arms. Often they had stolen glimpses of him in the washhouse and felt the strength of his young, muscular frame— yes, even with all its scars that crisscrossed his body like fine white lines—in the weakness of their loins.

They all glanced at the birds, and then someone muttered, "Well, what are *we* to do?"

Leborcham, the daughter of Oa and Adarc, glanced over at Ethne Ingubai. "It's an easy matter for you," she said petulantly. "But we do not have a Cúchulainn."

Ethne looked levelly at the women, hearing the envy in their voices, the reproach that she should have what every woman wanted. Then a great pity came over her and she nodded and said, "Well, then. If that is what you want, I will find my husband and give him your message."

"Ah, but you go too far," one of the others said quickly. " 'Tis not seemly that we should ask you to beggar yourself to your husband."

"I won't," Ethne said, and laughed. " 'Tis a terrible thing if that is the only way a woman can get her husband to do something for her."

Leborcham shrugged. "We are what we are—women. There's the ways of the men and the ways of the women. We use what we must in their world, and they use promises and good deeds in ours."

" 'Tis a pity you should think so," Ethne said.

"It isn't only me," Leborcham said, "but the other women as well. And if you won't ask him, then I will."

And so Leborcham went to Cúchulainn, who was lounging beside the lake, idly flipping small pebbles into the shallows and watching the concentric circles form and lap against the shore. There was *something* within those circles, but he couldn't quite grasp it. He felt it deeply within him, a yearning, a dark ache that pulled at him, making him want to enter the mirrored image that formed once the circles had finished. She stood a short distance away staring at him, puzzled for a moment, for there was a strange, melancholic expression upon his face that stirred uneasily within her. Then she stepped forward, calling his name, and he looked up, the expression replaced by a warmth that made her tingle. She nodded toward the birds and said, "The Ulster women have seen those as well."

He glanced out over the lake and smiled. "They are beautiful, aren't they? I have never seen birds like them before."

"Neither have we," she said. He turned his eyes upon her, and she felt giddy and faint. "I think the women would be pleased if you could gather the birds for them."

He frowned then, and touched his sword, the great Cruaidin Calidcheann, and made to draw it. For a brief moment she felt the terror that Cúchulainn's enemies feel when they see him draw that mighty blade; then she calmed herself.

He shook his head, his hand clenching angrily around the haft of his sword. "Tell me," he said. "Are the women of Ulster so arrogant that they think I will come at the hook of their finger? Can't they find anyone else to give them their bird hunt today?"

Leborcham frowned and straightened and stared with disapproval at the warrior. "Why do you rant and rage against us? It's most unseemly. Because of you, the women have developed one of their three blemishes.[2] They are blind to all other warriors when you are around—even their husbands. 'Tis little enough that you can do for them by gathering those birds."

Now the women of Ulster had three blemishes that caused them disfigurement: walking crookedly, stammering, and blindness. Those who loved Conall Cernach developed a meandering walk that did not allow them to proceed in a straight line, while those who loved Cúscraid Menn Macha, the One Who Stammers, stammered when they spoke. Those who loved Cúchulainn became blind in one eye, for when Cúchulainn underwent a warp-spasm, which when he was angry transformed him into a terrifying monster, one eye would sink into his head so far that the long bill of a crane could not reach it while the other eye would bulge and grow as large as a caldron in which a calf could be cooked.

Cúchulainn eyed her steadily for a moment, then shook his head. "You go too far with your logic, Leborcham," he said. Then he laughed. "But if I am the cause of women developing their wandering eye, then I'll gather the birds for them." He glanced over at the rest of the Red Branch, still waiting impatiently for the arrival of Conall and Fergus. "There's not much else to do at the moment," he added.

He raised his voice and shouted for his charioteer. "Laeg! Harness the horses to the chariot!"

Laeg stirred himself from where he lay sleepily in the shade of a giant oak and opened one eye to gaze balefully at Cúchulainn. "What is it? What is it?" he asked. "The heat of the day is hard upon the pate, and you're standing out there in the full of it, yammering about harnessing the horses? 'Tis bad enough that you keep the men from easing the great thirst within their throats, now you want to go for a ride?"

Cúchulainn gestured mockingly at where the women of Ulster stood silently, watching to see if Leborcham would deliver on her promise. "The women have a great deed for us," he said. "We must gather the birds for their white shoulders."

"Birds? You wake me for *birds*?" Laeg said unbelievingly. " 'Tis certain I am now that the great sun has baked what little brains you have." He sighed and rose, ambling away from the tree and down to where the Gray of Macha and the Black of Saingleu stood near Cúchulainn's famed chariot, the Carbad Seardha.[3]

Cúchulainn climbed into the chariot, and they chased after the birds. The birds rose into the air, and Cúchulainn cast his sword at them in an arch that brought it back to his hand after stunning the birds so that they flapped at the water with their claws and wings. Laeg and Cúchulainn entered the water, seized the birds, and gave them to the women. Each woman received a pair of the birds except Ethne Ingubai.

Cúchulainn looked at her apologetically and said, "You're angry with me, aren't you?"

She smiled and shook her head. "No, I'm not angry with you. If it hadn't been for me, the women would not have the birds for their shoulders. That is enough for me, for I know that they want badly to wrap their legs around your waist and that you have no eyes for any but me. I do not have to share the birds with them because I do not share you with them."

Cúchulainn laughed. "All right. Don't be angry, and in the future any birds that draw your eye that come to Muirthemne Plain or to the Boyne shall be yours."

Not long after this they saw two birds flying over the lake linked together with a red-gold chain. Their song was gentle and pleasing to the air, and all the men fell asleep except Cúchulainn, who noticed their beauty. "Those," he decided, "are the birds for Ethne, who did not share in the division of the birds we caught."

He nudged Laeg with his foot. The charioteer opened his eyes and stared up at Cúchulainn.

"Rise, lazybones," Cúchulainn said. He pointed at the two birds. "There are the two birds I have promised for Ethne."

"Bird chasing," Laeg said crossly. "Haven't you something better to occupy your time? And mine?"

Cúchulainn nudged him again, and Laeg sighed and sat up, shielding his eyes with his hands and staring at the birds. "If you listen to me, you'll avoid going after those birds," he said. "There's something not quite right with them. They seem to have a special power about them. You can take other birds for Ethne that will be just as good on another day."

"They *do* seem a bit peculiar," Ethne agreed.

"They are only birds," Cúchulainn said. He looked hard at Laeg. "Are you suggesting that I should avoid birds now? Place a stone in my sling, Laeg!"

Laeg sighed, stooked a stone in Cúchulainn's sling, and handed it to him. Cúchulainn threw, but the cast missed the birds. He shook his head. "Alas," he said, placed another stone in his sling himself, and cast it at the birds but missed again.

"What's wrong with me?" he cried. "Since the day I first took up arms I have never missed a cast with my sling."

Angrily he seized his spear and threw it, and the spear passed through one of the birds' wings. The birds swooped together, then dropped lower and flew along the water, then dived beneath the lake.

Cúchulainn stared at the spot where the birds had disappeared, then shook his head angrily and walked along the shore until he came to a standing stone. He moved into the shade and sat with his back against the stone. At last sleep fell upon him, despite his anger and his uneasy soul.

It was then that two women came to him. One of them wore a green mantle, while the other had a five-folded purple mantle. He admired their generous forms, the push of their breasts, the smooth curve of their hips. The woman in green came up to him, placed her hands on her full hips saucily, and laughed at him. Then she took a horsewhip and lashed him. The woman in purple came and laughed as well and lashed him. And then they took turns whipping him. Huge welts appeared on his body, and although he tried to awaken and defend himself, he could not. At last they departed, leaving him nearly dead.

The men of Ulster awakened then, saw the dreadful state of Cúchulainn, and went immediately to awaken him, but Fergus stopped them, saying, "No! You know that one may not awaken Cúchulainn until he awakens himself. It is a *geis* upon him that will bring death to he who awakens him. Besides, can't you see that this is only a vision?"

Soon Cúchulainn awoke by himself, groaning as he felt the pain lash through him.

"Who did this to you?" the Red Branch warriors demanded. But he was unable to speak.

Finally he managed to say, "Carry me to the sickbed in An Téte Brecc. Not to Dun Imrith or Dun Delgan."

Laeg frowned. "Won't you let us carry you to Dun Delgan, your fortress, where you can be helped by Emer?"

"No," Cúchulainn said firmly. "Take me to An Téte Brecc. It is there that I must go."

So they carried him to An Téte Brecc, where he languished for a full year, during which time he did not speak with anyone about what had happened to him.

Now upon a certain day just before the end of that year before Samhain, the warriors gathered around Cúchulainn in the house where he lay. Fergus stood by the wall, Conall Cernach by the bedrail, Lugaid Red Stripes by the pillow, and

Ethne Ingubai by his feet. While they were there a man entered the house and sat near the door to the room where Cúchulainn lay in his bed.

"What are you doing here? What do you want?" Conall asked suspiciously.

"That's not hard to answer," the man said. "If that man"— he nodded at Cúchulainn—"were healthy, he would guarantee my safety in this house. Since he is weak and wounded, his guarantee is made just that much stronger."

"Riddles," Conall growled. "Everyone wants to speak in riddles at times like this. Speak plainly, man, for I'm a plain-spoken man myself."

"I'm not afraid of you," the man said, "for I haven't come to banter or trade insults with you—it would be like dueling with an unarmed person anyway—but I have come to speak to that man."

Conall started to retort angrily, but the others stopped him.

"Speak to him if you can do any good to him," Lugaid said.

The man nodded and rose to his feet and went to stand over Cúchulainn.

"Cúchulainn, I speak to you of your sickness
And must tell you that your greatness
In this case will not in the least matter
For you can be healed only by Aed Abrat's daughters.

This has been said in Mag Cruach by Liban
While standing to the right of Labraid Lúathlám
Who said, 'Fand's heart has left her husband and gone
To you and she now wishes to lie with Cúchulainn.

'Joyous will be the day of Cúchulainn,' says Fand.
'When Cúchulainn comes alone to my land.

I will give him much silver and gold
And he will drink wine in his goblet gold.

If only he could love Manannan's Fand
This Cúchulainn, son of Sualdam!
Often I have seen him in slumber
Without his arms being encumbered.

'Tis to Mag Muirthemne he must go
On the night of Samhain and I will show
That no harm will come to him. Liban
Will come to heal the sickness of Cúchulainn.

Cúchulainn! Your illness will not last
Long if you will come to me as fast
As you can. If you were here, you would
Be healed by the daughters or Aed Abrat.' "

"Enough of this," growled Conall. "Tell us your name."

The man smiled at them and said, "I am Aengus, the son of Aed Abrat." Then he left as mysteriously as he had appeared, and all the men of Ulster looked at each other wonderingly.

"This ain't good," Conall said, scrubbing his thick knuckles through his hair in frustration. " 'Tis magic in the air that bodes no good for anyone."

Then Cúchulainn abruptly sat up, and all the men looked at him, forgetting the words of Conall.

"This is fortuitous," Lugaid said. "Now, can you tell us what has happened to you?"

He shook his head wearily. "I'm not certain. Last year at Samhain I had a vision."

"A vision?" Conall repeated.

"A dream, then, if you will," Cúchulainn said. And he told them what he had seen while asleep, about the woman in green and the woman in purple and what they had done to him and his powerlessness to raise himself from the deep sleep into which he had fallen.

" 'Tis as I said," Conall said, nodding his huge head. "No good comes of magic."

"Oh be quiet," Lugaid snapped. "What can we do, Cúchulainn?"

Cúchulainn shook his head. "I'm not certain." He looked at Conchobor, who had entered the room. "Do you have any answer for me?"

Conchobor shook his head. "You must go back to where you first dreamed the dream that made you into this. Rise and go now to the pillar where this happened."

Cúchulainn rose painfully from his sickbed and made his way to the pillar. As he leaned against it, the woman in green approached him, smiling. "This is good that you came, Cúchulainn," she said. She touched his arm gently.

He shook his head. "It wasn't good what happened to me here last year. Why did you do that to me?"

"It wasn't to harm you," she protested. "We did that to seek your friendship. That is all. I have come to speak to you on behalf of Fand, the daughter of Aed Abrat: Manannan Mac Lir has left her, and she has passed her love on to you. I am Liban, and I bring you a message from my husband, Labraid Lúathlám ar Cladeb.[4] He will send Fand to you if you will fight one day for him against Senach Saborth and Echu Iuil and Éogan Indber."

Cúchulainn shook his head. "I cannot fight today," he said. "I am in no shape to swing a sword."

She shook her head. "That will last only a little while," she said. "Then you will be as you were before the sickness and wasting came upon you. All the strength that you lost will be returned doubled to you. Labraid shall bestow that upon you as a gift, for he is the best of all warriors in all the world."

"Where will this happen?" Cúchulainn asked.

"In Mag Mell," Liban said. "And now I want to go to that other land."

Cúchulainn shook his head. " 'Tis once fooled I was, and no fool is as much a fool as the second fool. Let Laeg, my charioteer, travel with you and bring word back to me about what he sees and hears."

"Let him come then," Liban said. "But I would think that a hero such as yourself would not be passing the trip off onto another."

But Laeg went with her, and they traveled to Mag Mell, where Fand waited. When they arrived, Liban took Laeg and placed him beside her, holding on to his shoulder.

"What's this?" Laeg asked suspiciously.

"You must stay here today under my protection," Liban said.

Laeg shook his head. "I don't place myself under the protection of any woman. 'Tis not a seemly thing for a warrior to be under the guard of a woman."

"Men," she said, stamping her shapely foot. "Oh, if only Cúchulainn were here! He wouldn't have this false sense of pride."

"You wish for nothing more than I do," Laeg said. "I also wish he was here in my place." He looked around suspiciously, noting the beauty of the plain and noting that what seemed real was not real but only imaginary for mortal eyes.

They moved forward until they came to a lake. In the distance was an island, and a bronze skiff came across the lake toward them. They entered the boat and crossed over to the island. There they found a doorway, and a man appeared and waited silently upon them. Liban spoke:

> "Where is Labraid, he of the swift blade
> Who leads the army of victory? Laeg

Is here to see the man whose chariot brings
Victory always with his spears red-stained."

And the man replied to her, saying:

"Labraid, the swift sword-handler,
Is making ready his warriors
For the great battle that is certain to come
That will fill Mag Fidga with the slaughter of some."

They entered the house then, and saw a hundred and fifty couches, each with a woman lying upon it. All the women greeted Laeg:

"We give you greetings, mighty Laeg!
'Tis certain your quest means no peg
Grows between your legs! 'Tis best
As well that you remain our guest!"

Liban grinned at him. "Well, Laeg? What will you do now? Will you speak with Fand?"

Laeg tore his eyes from the women upon the couches and said, "I will if I can find her."

"That isn't hard," Liban said. "She is in her room, apart from the rest of the women."

They went to Fand's room to greet her, and she welcomed Laeg as the other women had welcomed her. Fand was the daughter of Aed Abrat, that is, fire of eyelash, for the pupil is the fire of the eye. Fand is the name of the tear that runs from the eye, and it was because of her purity and beauty that she was given that for her name, for no other name would suffice.

Now while they were visiting in her room, they heard the rattle of Labraid's chariot coming to the island. Liban said, "The spirit of Labraid is gloomy today. He sounds angry."

"Angry?" Laeg said apprehensively.

Liban nodded. "But don't worry. I'm with you. Now let's go and visit with him."

Reluctantly, Laeg rose and followed her outside, where Liban welcomed Labraid, saying,

> "Welcome, Labraid, mighty sword-handler
> Heir to an army of great spear-handlers
> Who hacks shields apart and scatters spears
> And cleaves bodies in half with sword and spear
> And slaughters free men! You seek bloody battles
> And always shine brightly when you rattle
> Your sword against your shield. The host
> Will always follow you who slay the most."

But Labraid did not reply to her. His face carried the look of a thundercloud, and she spoke again:

> "Welcome, Labraid, swift and bold
> Who is generous to all! Stories are told
> Of your greatness, your scars, your strong hand
> And your wisdom in judgment among your band.
> Swift is your vengeance, grim are your deeds
> In battle for your people. Such is your creed!"

Still Labraid made no answer. Liban frowned and tried again, saying:

> "Welcome, Labraid, who is not youth
> Pretending greatness. Any youth
> Can pretend to be strong
> But only you can belong
> To the din of war and lay low
> Your enemies with one blow!"

"You brag too much, woman," Labraid said, scowling.

"You'll find no arrogance in me
And no magic is used by me
Against others. Now we must go
To war against those who show
Mighty spears and red swords in hands
Red with blood from slaying bands
Of men in battle. There is much concern
About the outcome of this war. You'll learn
That there's no pride in me, woman,
For I must fight Echu Iuil, the man
Who brings multitudes against us
With all intention of slaying us!"

He glanced at Laeg and frowned, and looked questioningly at the woman Liban.

"Now let your mind be at ease," she said hastily. "This is Laeg, the charioteer to Cúchulainn, who has sent word that if all is as I have claimed he will come and join your army."

"Welcome, Laeg," Labraid said. "For the sake of the woman who has brought you here and for whom you have come, I bid you welcome! I do wish, however, that Cúchulainn was here in your place."

"No more than I do," muttered Laeg.

"Return now," Labraid said. "Go back to your own land. Liban will follow you."

So Laeg returned to Emain and told what he had seen to Cúchulainn and the other warriors who waited with him. Cúchulainn sighed and rose from his place. He passed his hand over his face and greeted Laeg like the Cúchulainn of old, for his mind was greatly strengthened by what he learned.

Now while this was happening, the three provinces of Erin came together in Temhair to seek one whom they could make the High King. There had not been a High King since the death of Conaire at Da Derga's Inn.[5]

The kings all met at Cairbre Niafer, and among them were Ailell of Connacht with his wife, Maeve, Curoi, and Tigernach, son of Luchta, king of Tuathmumain, and Finn Mac Ross, king of Leinster. But they would not ask the men of Ulster to help them in selecting a king, for all of them held grudges against the Red Branch.

A bull-feast was made for the Druids, much as in the time of Conaire, for the holding of an *imbas forasnai* in which the dreamer beheld a vision of the best man suited to be the High King. This time the dreamer saw a young man with a fine form, handsome, with two red stripes running down his body. He was sitting over a man wasting away in Emain Macha. Immediately a messenger was sent to Emain Macha to seek out the man who had been indicated by *imbas forasnai*.

At this time the men of Ulster were gathered around the sickbed of Cúchulainn, their hearts heavy with the weakness of the great champion. When the messenger came into the room, they all looked up, hopeful that he was from the Otherworld, bringing a way to stop the wasting of Cúchulainn. But the messenger passed by all of them and went directly to Conchobor and his chiefs. After he delivered his message, Conchobor cleared his throat apologetically and looked at the others in the room. "There is a young man with us, of good form and birth, who answers to the description given to those at the bull-feast to select the High King," he said.

"Without Ulster being there?" Conall asked. His heavy brows lowered in a threatening frown. "What is being played here, eh? Fox and geese? Seems to me like a move to come against the Red Branch."

Loegaire looked at him and grinned. "Who would have thought there was a devious mind behind that thick skull?" he said.

Conall's face turned dull red, and he lifted a huge fist threateningly. "Who—"

"Enough," Conchobor snapped. "The one that was seen in the vision was Lugaid Mac Clothru, Cúchulainn's pupil. He is sitting with his teacher caring for him."

And when it was made clear to Cúchulainn that the messengers had come for Lugaid to make him the High King in Temhair, Cúchulainn rose up and said:

> "Do not be a frightened man in battle.
> Do not be light-minded, hard to find, or proud.
> Do not be ungentle or hasty or passionate.
> Do not become drunken with your new richness like a flea drowned in the ale of a king's house.
> Do not scatter many feasts to strangers.
> Do not visit those who cannot receive you as a king.
> Do not let wrongful possession stand because it has lasted long, but rely upon those witnesses who know the rightful owner of land.
> Let tellers of history tell truth before you.
> Let the lands of brothers and their children be set down in their lifetime.
> If a family has increased in its branches, is it not from the same stem?
> Let them be called up and old chains again be established by oaths.
> Let the heir be left in lawful possession of the lands of his forefathers.
> Let strangers be driven from lands they do not own.
> Do not use too many words.
> Do not speak loudly.
> Do not mock.
> Do not insult.
> Do not make little of old people.

Do not think badly about anyone.

Do not ask for what is difficult to give.

Make a law of lending.

A law of oppression.

A law of pledging.

Listen to the advice of the wise and keep in mind the advice of the old.

Follow the rules of your fathers.

Do not be cold to friends and be strong toward your enemies.

Do not repay evil with evil in battles.

Do not speak too much.

Do not speak any harm of others.

Do not waste.

Do not scatter.

Do not do away with what is your own.

When you do wrong, receive the blame willingly.

Do not surrender the truth to any man.

Do not always seek to be the first, for that will make you jealous.

Do not be an idler so you become weak.

Do not ask too much that you may be thought little.

"Are you willing to follow this advice, my son?"

And Lugaid, who had been listening solemnly to the words of the great Cúchulainn, said, "As long as all is well, I will keep your words close to my heart and everyone will know that there is nothing wanting in me. I will do all that can be done."

Then Lugaid left with the messengers for Temhair, and there he was made king and he slept in Temhair that night. And after all had been done to make the High King, the people returned to their homes.

ii.

This portion was apparently written or transcribed by a different individual. Although it appears to be founded upon the same legend, there seems to be more of the sense of the romantic to it than in the former story with its Otherworld references. In this story we discover that Cúchulainn is still upon his sickbed and directs Laeg to go to the Otherworld. He does not seem to have met Liban for the second time, and he is now at Emain Macha and not An Téte Brecc. Emer is solely mentioned as Cúchulainn's wife, suggesting that the Ethne of the first section must have been only a "year's wife." This story seems to be far better organized than the previous story. It would appear that we had roughly two accounts of the same story linked rather precipitously by the election of Lugaid Red Stripes. This was probably done to provide the details of Cúchulainn's sickness, which would account as well for the repetition within the story.

Now it happened that Cúchulainn called Laeg to him and commanded him, saying, "Go, Laeg, to where Emer is and tell her that the fairy women have come hard upon me and destroyed my strength. Tell her that I seem to be getting better hour by hour and ask her to come and see me."

And Laeg, wishing to ease the mind of Cúchulainn, said:

> "Why are you engaging in this great folly
> And lying under a wasting sickness with a holly
> Branch waving to cool you? You are giving
> In to the wants of a wanton woman and living

The life that she wants from you like a dog
Who clings to the one who binds him and flogs
Him and tortures him to destroy his spirit.
Awake! Why lie here and let a woman spit
Upon your honor? Awake and let
Your valor shine brilliantly. I'll bet
You recover fully once you forget the sighs
Of that panting woman with the shapely thighs.
Once again you'll be able to perform deeds
When Labraid calls for you. He needs
You to join him in the coming war.
Rise up, for you are a warrior to the core!"

And after saying that Laeg departed and went to the place where Emer waited. He told her how Cúchulainn was in poor shape. Emer listened politely, then said:

"Alas, Laeg Mac Riangabra, that you should
Have visited the Otherworld in the wood
And come away without a cure
For the son of Deichtine's specter.

Shame upon the Red Branch men who could
Be searching the dark world in brotherhood
For the sake of their friend Cúchulainn
Who for them would have left no stone unturned.

If Fergus had fallen into that deep sleep
That a Druid's magic could keep
Away, then Cúchulainn would not rest
Until the Druid had done his best.

Or if Conall fell to napping
From his wounds that were sapping

His strength, you know that the Hound
Would search until a doctor he found.

If Loegaire Buadabach faced the danger
Of death from a wound at the hands of a stranger
Cúchulainn would search the meadows of Ériu
For a doctor to cure the son of Connad Iliu.

If Celtchair of the deceits had some
Sleep that made a long wasting come
Sétanta would travel day and night
Until he found the *sídhe* with the light.

If Furbade of the Fan were laid low
For a long time from a hard blow
Cúchulainn would search the hard earth
Until the needed cure he unearthed.

The dead but undead hosts of *Sídhe Truim*
Have dispersed their deeds to redeem
Themselves, but the *sídhe* sleep
Has seized the Hound. Weep! Weep!

Your sickness touches me deeply with
Knowing how you fare, Hound of Conchobor's smith.
My heart and mind are troubled when
I wonder how I might heal him. Then

My heart pumps blood in vain
For the wasting of the horseman of the plain.
He must come here, to his home and me
From the Mag Muirthemne assembly.

I am afraid that we are parted
By a specter that has started

An evilness. My voice is weak
Because of his illness. I cannot speak

Of how it must be to not sleep together
For a month, a season, a year. Together
We should be, for I long to hear
His pleasing voice close to my ear."

But Cúchulainn could not make the trip to her, so Emer
went to Emain to visit him. She sat upon his bed and scolded
him, saying, "Shame on you, lying there for the love of a
woman! If you stay long in bed, you will become even sicker
than you are now."

Then she said:

"Rise, warrior from red Ulster
From your sleep and bolster
Our failing hearts. Arise hale
And hearty from your deep vale

Of sleep and see your king and
His shoulder filled with crystal and
His splendid drinking horns and
His chariots racing the sun and

See his ranks of *fidchell* men.
See his ranks of hearty champions.
See the tall and gentle women
See his lusty queens and men.

See all the wonders of autumn, bold
Colors in the trees and the coming cold
Of winter. And see that as you should
And not as those you serve in the wood

Of the Otherworld. Deep sleep makes depression
And weariness follows the heels of oppression.
Long sleep moves upon one with stealth
And makes one weak, near to death.

Throw off this sleep and come to me
And know the peace you long to see.
Many gentle words have been spoken
To you. Come! Arise! Give us a token.

Cúchulainn rose shakily then, and passed his hand over his face and threw off all weariness. He rose and went to Airbe Rofir. There Liban came to him and invited him to the *sidhe.* He shook his head and said, "Where does Labraid live?"

"Not difficult that to say," she answered.

"Labraid dwells upon a clear lake
Where many women visit for the sake
Of their beauty. If you decide to find
Him, you will not become blind

To his mighty arm that hews
Hundreds at one blow. Through
Him you will meet the woman
In the purple cloak. This woman

Is the one you have seen. Labraid will
Give her to you for helping him. Still
You must fight greatly alongside
Him and from his enemies guard his side

As he slays many with his red
Sword, breaks spears, crushes shields

Of those foolish hosts who would try
To seize his lands from him or die.

He is worthy of you, there can be no
Doubt of that. His eyes are bright and glow
With more honor than others in the *sídhe*
For none has shown more valor than he.

His fame is greater by far than those
Who follow him. His warriors stay close
To him but still they cannot match his deeds
For they are legion. His mighty steeds

Join with him in battle, wearing gold
Upon their bridles, and with bold
Hooves carry him past the surging swells
Of the sea to the house where he dwells."

But Cúchulainn felt uneasy and replied, "I will not go upon
a woman's invitation."

She smiled. "Afraid, Cúchulainn? Very well. Then let Laeg
come and see everything and come back and tell you the truth
about what he has seen. If you will not trust me, surely you
will trust your own charioteer. And he will be safe, for charioteers are guarded by the words of Labraid."

And Laeg went with Liban to Mag Lúada and An Bile
Búada, over Óenach nEmna and into Óenach Fidgai, and there
they found Aed Abrat and his daughters. Fand greeted Laeg
and asked, "But where is Cúchulainn? Why has he not come
himself? Don't misunderstand me—you are welcome—but I
was waiting for the Hound to come to me."

"He would not come upon a woman's beckoning," Laeg
answered. "Not unless he was certain that the invitation came

from you and was not a trick to bring him forever into the Otherworld."

Fand smiled happily at this, for she thought she could sense Cúchulainn's love behind Laeg's words. "Return to him, then," she said, "and tell him that the invitation did indeed come from me. But"—she frowned—"go at once, for the battle is today and he is badly needed."

Laeg returned hastily to Cúchulainn, and when Cúchulainn asked him, "How does it look, Laeg?" the charioteer answered,

"It is time to go, for today
Is the day of the battle. I say
That I arrived to find the place
A wonder, and in the space

Of time I came to a mound
And among the warriors I found
Labraid waiting, sitting with thousands
Of weapons around him. Like sand

Was his hair and tied back with a gold
Apple. He recognized me by my bold
Five-folded crimson cloak. 'Will you
Come with me to Failbe the Fair's house?'

In the house were two kings meeting,
Failbe the Fair and Labraid, waiting
With a hundred fifty warriors, and
They lived together there as a band.

On the right side of the house fifty beds
Waited for as many warriors. And fifty beds
Waited on the left for warriors. The beds
Have round columns and instead

Of carved wood are inlaid with gold.
They gleam brightly, I am told
From light that comes from a stone,
A precious and brilliant stone.

At the door toward the west
Where the light from the sun is best
Stands a troop of gray horses with dappled manes
And another troop of horses with brown manes.

At the door toward the east are three
Trees of purple glass. In the tree
Tops flocks of birds sing sweet
Songs to the children beneath their feet.

At the door to the house is a tree
Of silver, but before the sun I see
It turn to gold and beautiful harmony
Comes from the branches of the tree.

Three score trees are there as well
And each tree bears fruit that swells
And ripens, and a hundred men eat
Of the fruit as a wonderful treat.

A vat of rich mead stands as well
In the house and is always full
And within the house a woman
Lives more beautiful than a woman

From Erin. She has yellow hair
And blue eyes that can stare
Lovingly at you. Full of charm
And grace, she means you no harm.

This woman said, 'Who are you?
I do not recognize you. Who
Has come in the place of Cúchulainn?
Are you a servant of that man?'

I went very slowly to her, fearing
For my honor, but her bearing
Caused my fears to flee when she
Asked, 'Will he come to me?'

A pity that you did not go
Yourself, for then you would know
What I know about that land
Which is better than any other land."

"This is good," Cúchulainn said. "I am grateful that you would go there and bring back such glad tidings."

Laeg shrugged. "Perhaps. But I think that you need to go and see for yourself." And he spoke again about what he had seen:

"I saw a bright and noble land
Where falsehoods are unknown.
There lives the king Labraid
Whose people are well-led.

While passing across Mag Lúada
I was shown An Bile Búada.
At Mag Denda I managed to take
A pair of two-headed snakes.

As we were together, Liban said,
'I wish you were Cúchulainn instead.'

And then I saw the lovely Fand
More beautiful than any in the land.

I could continue about that madame
And others who descended from Adam,
But none would I find as pretty as Fand
Who has no equal in Erin's land.

I saw warriors slashing with spears.
I saw women feasting without fear.
I saw the beauty of their daughters.
I saw the red of bloody slaughter.

I saw beauty without compare
And I looked everywhere.
But this I tell you truly:
Fand is the only beauty

Who could deprive the fierce troops
Of their senses. Her breasts are scoops
Of fresh fallen snow. Her lips as red
As a rose. Rise up, now, from your bed!"

And Cúchulainn rose and went to that land that Laeg had
spoken about in such glowing terms. He took with him his
chariot, and when he arrived at the island, Labraid greeted him
enthusiastically and the women made him welcome as well.
Fand was waiting to give him a special welcome.

"What now?" Cúchulainn asked after enjoying Fand's lips.

"Not hard that," Labraid said, grinning. "We will take a
turn around the enemy and see what we can see."

They rode together around the host, and the numbers
seemed endless. Labraid shook his head. "There are more of
them than I thought," he confessed. He sighed.

Cúchulainn said, "Go away now, and leave me here alone to think."

Labraid nodded and left Cúchulainn behind. Two Druid ravens came down to the enemy and told them that Cúchulainn was near. The warriors were angry and said, "No doubt this is the warped one from Erin." And because they were angry at the news the ravens brought to them, they chased them away so that they found no resting place in that land.

Early the next morning, Eochaid Íuil rose and stumbled out to the spring to bathe his face and hands. When he raised the water to his face, Cúchulainn saw an opening beneath his tunic and hurled his spear. The spear struck Eochaid and went through him.

Others heard his cries of distress and pain and rushed to aid him. Cúchulainn slew thirty-three of them before Senach the Unearthly rushed him. A furious battle raged back and forth as the other warriors stood back to let them fight. Then Senach dropped his guard, and Cúchulainn's sword came up and over and beheaded him.

As the others started to rush Cúchulainn, Labraid appeared in his war chariot and in three furious rushes broke the back of the army waiting. They turned and fled before the two, and when Cúchulainn made to follow them Labraid put out his hand to stop the wanton slaying of the Hound.

Cúchulainn turned toward him, the battle vision still upon him, his face a mask of horror, his muscles knotted and engorged with blood.

"Careful!" shouted Laeg. "When the blood is upon him, he may turn on us as well!"

Labraid pulled his arm back and looked questioningly at Laeg. "What should be done?" he asked.

"Have three vats of cold water brought quickly!" Laeg said. "The first vat into which he is placed will boil over; the second

will take the heat of the battle from him; but it needs the third
vat to cool his battle-self down."

Labraid did Laeg's bidding as quickly as possible, and when
Cúchulainn emerged from the last vat, his eyes clear, his skin
smooth and muscles relaxed, Fand sang:

> "Fidga's plain, where we shall assemble
> And all the land at the trampling trembles
> As this young and beardless youth rides
> This eve in the chariot he guides.
>
> Blood red the sky above him
> As his wheels go droning
> Over the land as fairies cry
> Their chants to the battle reply.
>
> His mighty horses leap beneath their traces
> And I admire their leaps, the grace
> With which they fly like the spring wind.
> They are not like others I can find.
>
> Fifty golden balls float high in the air
> From the breath of this hero. There
> Are kings who tremble at his approach
> And dare not offer his deeds reproach.
>
> The four dimples of his cheeks glow
> One in green, the other in blue
> One blood red, the warrior's due
> The other purple in hue.
>
> Seven lights flash from his eyes
> And all flinch from them and cry

Out in fear as his proud glance
Stabs them harshly like a lance.

Beardless, like a youth, his praise
Is sung throughout Erin and raises
The envy of all. Three shades of hair
Are coiled neatly, but none dare

To crop those locks as blood red
Runs his blade, a color dreaded
Below the silver hilt while his shield
Bears golden bosses and yields

Around its rim white bronze. War he
Seeks and his slaughter is high. See
Where heroes follow in his wake
For none dare his road to take.

We greet him, young Cúchulainn!
All of Aed Abrat's daughters throng
Together to welcome him home
No more the plains to roam.

The demon war is finished
And on his skin no blemish
Can be seen. Every tree stands
Stained with blood-rain from his hands."

But she was not alone in her praise as Liban chanted:

"Hail, mighty Cúchulainn, who came to our aid
From Muirthemne, where he could have stayed.
See how he rides, glorious, with a great heart
That beats battle bright. He stands apart

From other heroes. Firm like a rock he
Stands while waging war, and see
How mighty is his blood-rage
That causes men to flee despite his age.

Tell us now all the deeds you've done
This day under the blood-red sun
Mighty Cúchulainn. We wait eagerly
To hear your tales! Don't be beggarly!

Come and sing about battles won
This day, tell us all you have done
To save our land from darkness
Visible and to your deeds confess."

Cúchulainn grinned at her, and all the maidens who saw
his smile felt their hearts lurch in their breasts and their loins
ache from want. He took a deep breath, then chanted:

"From my hand flew my spear that I cast.
Through the host of Stream-Yeogan it passed.
I did not know, however, the fame I'd won
Or who my victim was, what deed I'd done.

Who's to tell if his hand was greater than mine?
That is given to the past and I cannot divine
The answer. He hid in a mist and could not see
My cast, my sword, he did not see me

Before he died. Warriors came on every side
Of me then. Upon blood-red steeds did they ride.
They came from Manannan, the sea god, those foes
And from their throats a battle-cry rose.

I heard Eochaid Íuil's death rattle come
From his lips and knew that he was done
With life. Yet I swear that it was no great deed
That I threw and spilled upon the ground his life-seed."

And after he had finished his telling of his tale, Fand took him by his hand and led him eagerly to bed. They lay together for a full month, but at the end of that time Cúchulainn bade her farewell. She held his arm, however, when he tried to part and said, "Tell me where I can come to meet you again. Pick a place. I'll be there."

He smiled at her and said, "Do you know the Strand of the Yew-Tree's Head?" She nodded. "There I will meet you when the moon is full."

Now Emer heard about the tryst that they had made, and anger filled her, a red rage that made her hands shake as she sharpened knives for fifty women to take with her as she went to the place where Cúchulainn meant to lay with Fand. When she came to the yew tree, however, she found Cúchulainn and Laeg playing *fidchell,* and they did not see her approach until Fand shouted, "Laeg! What is that coming toward us?"

"Where?" Laeg asked, looking up, blinking as he took his thoughts from the game.

"There!" Fand said, and pointed toward Emer and the fifty women as they approached.

"What is this, Laeg, that I see coming?
Fifty well-ranked women bearing
Upon their breasts bright pins of gold
And in their hands gleaming knives they hold.
Here comes, I think, Forgall's daughter
Leading all of them to their slaughter."

Cúchulainn spoke, saying, "Do not fear
Their coming! You'll shed no tear

Of hurt from their hands. Come into my
Chariot and take a seat. Do not sigh
About what might be. Emer will not dare
To harm you with her rage. I'll be there
To stand between you and the daughters
That she leads intent upon your slaughter."

Then to Emer he said:

"I avoid coming against you, my lady
As heroes avoid friends in shady
Times of battle. The knife you hold
Shall not be used sated with Fand's blood."

"Speak!" Emer cried. "Tell me, Hound
Have you another woman found
To care for you? To cry for you? Why
Do you lay this shame upon me? Try
To make me understand
Why among all who dwell in this land
You have picked this woman from the *sídhe*
When among Erin's women you have me
As your wife? All here honor your deeds
But there are some things we cannot heed."

"Speak, Emer," said Cúchulainn, "tell me:
Why shouldn't I lie with this lady?
She is fair of form and bright and skilled
In many things. You can see how filled
She is with love for me. She is a good mate
For any, even the sea god she once sated
With her skill in lovemaking. But he
Is now caught up in matters with the sea

And no longer lays within her arms
And tarries awhile with her charms.

She has much wealth in steeds and
Cattle that roam the *sídhe* in large bands.
A dear wife she would be for any like me.
And I have taken her gift as such. The sea
Will roar with its loss as will you for the vow
I made you I now break and you shall now
Seek to find another champion but none
Will ever match my scars, the deeds I've done."

Great tears came to Emer's eyes. "You're wrong, Cúchulainn. The woman whose arm you hold is in no way better than me! You see things that are red as fair and what is white as something new and bright. But what is sweet can often taste sour after time has passed. What seems truth is often lies despite what you think is the wisdom of time itself! Once we lived together in honor and pride, and I think such would still be the way if she was away from your sight."

And Cúchulainn felt the pain of her loss, and his heart went out to her as he said, "By all the gods I promise that you will always find favor with me as long as life flows through my veins."

"You would leave me then?" cried Fand. Tears splattered against the front of her dress, and Emer took pity upon her and sighed. "No, it is far more fitting that I be the one left behind. After all, I have known his arms far longer than you," she said.

Fand studied her for a moment, then shook her head sadly. "No, it is I who must go, for I feel a great danger coming close upon me from a long ways away."

And at that moment a great lamentation set upon Fand, and her soul cried out against the shame of being deserted and

left to make her own way homeward. The mighty love she bore
Cúchulainn still raged deeply within her.

"I must go now for mighty need
Compels me to stay! I must heed
My word for others or become
A harridan baking in a sunless sun.

But how sweet it would be to stay
And remain in your arms all day!
Far sweeter than the Otherworld
Is the land of Ériu in your world.

Emer, you must take your man
And renew each the banns
You once made. My arms ache
For his embrace and love make.

Men have often come seeking me
From other places to my old sea-
Home but none could ever be
Like Cúchulainn is to me!

No woman should her longing set
On any man unless he has met
Her on equal grounds. I can see
However, that will never be.

You brought fifty women here today
To murder Fand or bring her to bay
And make her your captive. But
This will never happen. Shut

Your mind to revenge, woman
For I can call three times the men

If I need them. Now I'll leave
And take myself home to the sea."

Now while the confrontation between Fand and Emer was happening, Manannan Mac Lir saw that his wife was outnumbered by the mortal women and that Cúchulainn was about to scorn her for the love of his mortal wife. He came flying from the east, seeking his wife, and when he arrived only Fand could see his white hair and beard among all that were there. A great bitterness filled her and she sang:

"So. The son of the sea decides to come
From Yheogan the Stream and seek some
Woman for his wife? Once you were dear
To me as my husband. But you seared

My heart with pain when you left me
For other business upon the cold sea.
My noble heart is not filled with love
For you anymore. You have shoved

Me away from the ocean's side
Where once we could hide
From others and reside alone
In the sea we made our home.

Once I was Manannan's equal spouse
And the golden armlet sealed our vows
To each other. You were my lord and
Protector among all in that sea-land!

Two score and ten bridesmaids came
Through the heather wearing the same

Brave colors as the sun, the sea, the sky,
And I gave to you my own bounty

Of fifty men, and no frenzied strife
Existed between you and your wife
Where a hundred strong men led
Gladsome lives with the wives they wed.

Manannan draws near; I sense his speed
Over the ocean as I once fled
From his home. As a horseman he rides
The maned waves of the sea for his bride.

He has passed us near, now
But you cannot see or know how
He is to the fairies who worship him
And are willing to do all he bids them.

But know this, my Cúchulainn,
That I am weak and a woman
Who has loved a mortal dearly
And for that I can see I nearly

Lost my life to the hands of your wife.
I cannot live in a land of strife
And so I go and leave unsullied
Your honor complete and unharmed.

Ah, but this parting seems hard
Although my going is not barred.
Know this, Laeg: your insult was great
And I did not deserve that as my fate.

Now I leave to be again with my spouse
Alone in the sea where we made our house.

And so none can doubt my word, you see
I show you now, Manannan of the sea!"

And with that she rose into the air behind Manannan as he circled them. He greeted her politely, saying, "Well, my lady, what will you do? Go with me or stay here and wait until Cúchulainn decides to leave his wife and come to you?"

A tear spoiled the perfection of Fand's eye as she replied, "Either one of you makes a worthy spouse for a woman. Neither one is better than the other, yet, Manannan, I must go with you, for I cannot wait for Cúchulainn to make up his mind. He has betrayed me by choosing his wife over me. Besides, you have no consort worthy of you but myself."

Cúchulainn watched as Fand went from him to Manannan and cried out to Laeg, "What is this? Do you understand what is happening?"

"That's not hard to answer," Laeg said. "Fand is leaving with Manannan, her husband, since she has decided that she is not pleasing to your sight. Well," he added, "as pleasing as is your own wife."

Cúchulainn leaped three times high into the air with sorrow and made three leaps to the south, where he came to Tara Luachra. There he dwelt for a long time without meat or drink and sleeping alone on the high road that ran through the middle of Luachra.

Emer went to Emain Macha and there sought out Conchobor. She told Conchobor all that had happened and what Cúchulainn was going through. Conchobor immediately sent out his wise men and skilled people along with the main Druids of Ulster so that they might find Cúchulainn and tie him fast with deerhide thongs and bring him back to Emain Macha with them.

When Cúchulainn saw what they were going to do, he tried to kill them, but they chanted wizard and fairy songs against him, and when he fell into a daze they bound his feet and hands and would not release him until the wild frenzy had left him.

Then he begged for a drink, and the Druids made him a drink of forgetfulness so that he would have no more memory of Fand and the Otherworld, and they gave the same drink of forgetfulness to Emer so that she would lose the jealousy she carried in her heart, for by now her state was no better than that of Cúchulainn.

And Manannan shook his cloak between Cúchulainn and Fand so that they might never meet together in this world or, for that matter, eternity.

Appendix A

Structures in ancient Irish poetry

A quick summation of Ancient Irish poetry can probably be made best by recalling Kuno Meyer's work, *Ancient Irish Poetry* (London, 1913):

> Slowly, ... the fact is becoming recognized in ever wider circles that the vernacular literature of ancient Ireland is the most primitive and original among the literatures of Western Europe, and that in its origins and development it affords a most fascinating study. Whatever may be its intrinsic merit, its importance as the earliest voice from the dawn of West European civilization cannot be denied.
>
> It was only on the outskirts of the Continental world, and beyond the sway and influence of the Roman Empire, that some vigorous nations preserved their national institutions intact, and among them there are only three whom letters reached early enough to leave behind some record of their pagan civilisation in a vernacular literature. These were the Irish, the Anglo-Saxons, and, comparatively late-comers, the Icelanders.
>
> It was during this period [fourth century on] that the oral literature, handed down by many generations of bards and story-tellers, was first written down in the monasteries. Unfortunately, not a single tale, only two or three poems, have come down to us from these early centuries in contemporary manuscripts. In Ireland itself most old books were destroyed during the Viking terror which burst upon the island at the end of the eighth century. But, from the eleventh century onward, we have an almost unbroken series of hundreds of manuscripts, in which all that had escaped destruction was collected and arranged. Many of the tales and poems thus preserved were undoubtedly originally composed in the eighth century; some few perhaps in the seventh; and as the Irish scholarship advances, it is not unlikely that fragments of poetry will be found which, from linguistic or internal evidence, may be claimed for the sixth century.

The purely lyrical poetry of ancient Ireland may be roughly divided into two sections—that of the professional bard attached to the court and person of a chief; and that of the unattached poet, whether monk or itinerant bard.

Religious poetry ranges from single quatrains to lengthy compositions dealing with all the varied aspects of religious life. Many of them give us a fascinating insight into the peculiar character of the early Irish Church, which differed in so many ways from the rest of the Christian world.

In Nature poetry the Gaelic muse may vie with that of any other nation. Indeed, these poems occupy a unique position in the literature of the world. To seek out and watch and love Nature, in its tiniest phenomena as in its grandest, was given to no people so early and so fully as to the Celt. Many hundreds of Gaelic and Welsh poems testify to this fact.

Of ancient love-songs comparatively little has come down to us. What we have are mostly laments for departed lovers.

The commonest stanza is a quatrain consisting of heptasyllabic lines with the rhyme at the end of the couplet.

Basic rules seemed to dictate that a peculiar device be used: the poem ending with the same word or line that begins it. Additionally, end rhymes and internal rhymes occasionally find their way into the poetry, but the most common form seems to be a type of chain alliteration, which would, in the case of an oral tradition, provide a check for the bard performing the piece.

Here are the forms:

Ae Freislighe: A quatrain stanza with each line containing seven syllables. Lines 1 and 3 rhyme in triple rhymes, while lines 2 and 4 rhyme in double rhymes.

Caasbairdne: A quatrain stanza of heptasyllabic lines with lines 2 and 4 rhyming and lines 1 and 3 consonate with them. There are at least (but by no means only) two cross-rhymes in each couplet. The first couplet, however, doesn't necessarily follow this pattern. The final syllable of line 4 alliterates with the preceding stressed word.

Deibhidhe: A quatrain stanza with seven syllables per line and light rhyming in couplets. Alliteration will be found between two words in each line, with the final word of line 4 alliterating with the preceding stressed word. There are at least two cross-rhymes between lines 3 and 4.

Droighneach: A very loose stanza form in which each line can have from nine to thirteen syllables and always ends in a trisyllabic word. There is some rhyming between lines 1 and 3, and lines 2 and 4, but this is not exact rhyme. Stanzas may have any number of quatrains within them, and there are at least two cross-rhymes in each couplet and alliteration in each line, with usually the final word alliterating with the preceding stressed word. This is always true of the last line.

Rannaicheacht Ghairid: A quatrain stanza with uneven lines, the first line with three syllables and the other three with seven. The stanza will rhyme *aaba,* with a cross-rhyme between lines 3 and 4.

Rannaicheacht Mhor: A quatrain stanza of heptasyllabic lines consonating *abab.* There are at least two cross-rhymes in each couplet, and the final word of line 3 rhymes with a word in the middle of line 4. In the second couplet the rhymes must be exact, but the first couplet may be closed.

Rionnaird Tri-Nard: A quatrain stanza of hexasyllabic lines with disyllabic endings. Lines 2 and 4 rhyme while line 3 consonates with them. There are two cross-rhymes in the second couplet but none in the first. There is alliteration in each line, and the last syllable of line 1 alliterates with the first accented word of line 2. There are two cross-rhymes in the second couplet.

Séadna: A quatrain stanza of alternating octosyllabic lines with disyllabic endings and heptasyllabic lines with monosyllabic endings. Lines 2 and 4 rhyme; line 3 rhymes with the stressed word preceding the final word of line 4. There are two cross-rhymes in the second couplet. There is alliteration in each line, the final word of line 4 alliterating with the preceding stressed word. The final syllable of line 1 alliterates with the first stressed word of line 2.

Appendix B

the healing rivers

And-sain dariachtatar óendóene
d'Ultaib and-so innossa d'fortacht &
d'forithin Conculaind, .i. Senal
Uathach & da mac Gégge .i.
Muridach & Cotreb. Acus rucsatar
leo é go glassib & go aibnib
Connaille Murthemne, do thuargain
& do nige a chneda & a chrechta,
(a) alaid & a ilgona i n-agthib na
srotha sain & na n-aband. Daíg
dabertis Tuatha De Danand lubi &
lossa ícce & slansen for glassib &
aibnib crichi Conailli Murthemne,
do fortacht & do forithin
Conculaind, comtís brecca barruani
na srotha díb.

Conid ed and-so anmanda na n-
aband legis sain Conculaind:

Sáis, Buáin, Buas, Bithlain,
Findglais, Gleóir, Glenamain, Bedg,
Tadg, Telaméit, Rind, Bir, Brenide,
Dichaem, Muach, Miliuc, Cumung,
Cuilend, Gáinemain, Drong, Delt,
Dubglass.

Then came certain men of the
Ulstermen thither to help and
succour Cuchulain. Before all,
Senoll Uathach and the two sons of
Gegè: Muridach and Cotreb, to wit.
And they bore him to the streams
and rivers of Conalle Murthemni,
to rub and to wash his stabs and
his cuts, his sores and his many
wounds in the face of these streams
and rivers. For the Tuatha De
Danann were wont to put herbs
and plants of healing and a curing
charm in the waters and rivers of
the territory of Conalle Murthemni,
to help and to succour Cuchulain,
so that the streams were speckled
and green-topped therewith.

Accordingly these are the names of
the healing rivers of Cuchulain:

Sas, Buan, Buas, Bithslan, Findglas
(Whitewater), Gleoir, Glenamain,
Bedg, Tadg, Telameit, Rind, Bir,
Brenidé, Dichaem, Muach, Miliuc,
Cumung, Cuilind, Gainemain,
Drong, Delt, Dubglas (Blackwater).

Appendix C

the pangs of the ulstermen

The *Cess Noinden Ulad* or *The Debility of the Ulaid* is one of the *remscéla* or preludes to the *Táin Bó Cuailngé*. It was apparently composed to explain why Cúchulainn had to stand alone against the raiding armies of Connacht when Maeve sought to capture the Brown Bull of Cooley. The tale also explains the naming of Emain Macha after an etymology that is found in the *Dinnshenchas*. It is, however, a typical tale and perhaps one of the earliest that explains the danger of love between a mortal and a being from the Otherworld. It may be found in *The Book of Leinster*.

T HERE LIVED AT THE TIME on the high hills and among the solitudes of Ulster a rich cow-lord who was called Crunuchu Mac Agnoman. He had accumulated much wealth over the years by dint of hard labor and shrewd bargaining. He remained in solitude because he had little time for the posturing and bragging that the other cow-lords engaged in, going his own way quietly, slowly making himself into one of the wealthiest ever.

During the time that he was building his wealth, he sired four sons, but the mother of his children suddenly died and his sons went on to their own families, leaving him alone on the hill where he had built his home.

One day while he was lying forlorn upon a couch, peering out through the doorway to the setting of the sun (at such times he felt the most lonely, for the beauty of the evening reminded him of the beauty of his wife), he saw a beautiful woman walking across the pasture toward his house. She was young and stately and bore herself proudly with great distinction.

Much to his astonishment, she entered the house without making herself known. He held his breath as he stared transfixed at her beauty. Her generous lips curved in a delicious smile that made him feel faint; then, without a word, she turned and cleaned the house (which had been carelessly kept with the death of his wife), drew a chair up to the hearth, and silently stirred the fire into a blaze.

Crunuchu tried to question her, but his tongue refused to form itself around the words he wanted to utter, and so he sat silently, watching her, wondering what she would do next. He did not have long to wait, for the woman rose and gathered a kneading-trough to make bread and a sieve and cooking pots to prepare the evening meal. Then, while the meal was cooking, she gathered a bowl and went out to milk the cow that was lowing miserably in the lean-to next to the house. When she returned, she still did not say a word but busied herself with the setting of the table and the placing of the food.

Then she went into his kitchen and gave further directions to his servants, who looked wonderingly at their master, but by now Crunnchu was caught up into the mystery himself and he shook his head, warning them not to ask questions.

'Tis a wonderful thing that has happened, he thought, and if I say anything, I may drive her away. A woman is usually spooked by too many questions. Yes, better to leave it until she says the first words.

She came in and smiled at him again and took a seat next to him as the servants bustled in and filled the table with a wondrous feast the likes of which Crunnchu had not seen in many a day.

After the meal, when all went to their couches for the night, the woman remained behind to smoor the fire. Then she came to Crunnchu's couch and lay down beside him, placing her hand intimately by his side. His throat felt dry, but a great excitement entered his loins, an excitement that he had not thought he would ever feel again.

"Who are you?" he managed, finally.

"My name is Macha," she said.

"And—" he began, but she placed a well-formed finger softly against his lips, silencing him. "Is that not enough for you in your loneliness?" she asked.

He wanted to ask how she knew of his loneliness and the name of her father, for he was afraid that she might have run away from her home—or, worse yet, from her husband—and for Crunnchu to take her in would be to bring down disaster upon his head and house. But he made the mistake of looking into her blue eyes and finding himself falling into their depths as if he had taken a tumble into a well.

Best not to question the gold tossed through the door, he thought; then his lips were silenced for certain when she pulled his head down and pressed hers to his.

And so they lived together happily and Crunnchu's herds grew even larger, and when he looked into a mirror, he thought he saw himself growing more handsome and—was he simply being foolish?—handsomer each day. But such was his happiness that Crunnchu silenced all his misgivings and took great joy in the good fortune that had befallen him.

Now frequently large fairs and assemblies or meetings and feasts were held around Ulster, and all the men and women found it worth their while to attend, for sometimes bargains could be had and fortunes earned if one kept his wits about him during such gatherings. Crunnchu had not gone to such a gathering in quite a spell since the death of his wife, but there

came a time when the king of the Red Branch held a feast-day and Crunnchu decided that he would like to attend it and show off his good fortune
to the others. But, strangely, his wife refused to go.'

"I really would like to go to the feasting at the king's hall," he said
one day over the midday meal. She looked at him, studying him closely,
then sighed. "I do not think it would be wise for you to go," she said. "You
run the danger of meeting some friends of yours and speaking about us."

"And what is wrong with that?" Crunnchu asked irritably. " 'Tis
proud I am of you, and a man is entitled to show off his wife to others. I
can seen them dripping with envy when they cast an eye upon you."

"Flatterer," she said, giving him a small smile. But it quickly slipped
from her lovely lips as she said: "But you must know that, by speaking
about us, you will bring the separation of us as well."

"I promise, then, not to utter a word," said Crunnchu. " 'Tis enough
if you're by my side, and we'll let the others take the thinking onto themselves what they will."

"Well—" she said doubtfully, furrowing her pretty brow in thought.

"Come, come," he insisted. "There'll be other women there to chat
with and wares to see and buy."

She shook her head. "All I need is here." She reached out to take his
hand, then heaved another sigh. "But I know that men cannot live only
with women but must have the company of others as well about them from
time to time. So we will go. But," she cautioned again, her face drawn into
serious lines, "be certain that you do not speak of what we have become,
for to talk about one's good fortune is certainly to lose it."

"I know. I know," he said, waving his hand in dismissal. "The gods
are fickle about such things. Though why they should be is beyond me. If
a man can boast about his killings, why can't he boast about his beddings?"

And so they left it at that, and when the time came for the festival,
they left together for the Red Branch Hall.

This festival was far better than others, the colors of the tents and
clothes far more brilliant than Crunnchu ever remembered, the horses sleek
and fit, the races, combats, tournaments, games, and processions more involved and trying than ever before.

When the ninth hour came the king's chariot was brought forward,
drawn by a pair of beautiful night-black horses, and races were held around
the fortress. But no other horses came close to defeating the king's.

After the last race was run and no other warriors seemed willing to
try their luck against the king's horses, the bards came forward to sing
their songs in praise of the king and queen, the poets and Druids that were
in his household.

"Never have two horses been so miraculously foaled as those of the king's we have seen in this festival! In all of Erin, there can be no others that can defeat them!"

Now Crunnchu had been sampling the wine and beer, especially an autumn mead sweet with honey, and when he heard the bragging of the people on the king's horses, he scoffed, drew a hand across his mouth, and said, "Ah now, they're not as fast as all that. My wife could beat the pair of them handily."

Much to his dismay, the king was passing at the moment, and when he heard Crunnchu's words, he whirled about, brow furrowing angrily, and said, "Bring that man to me!"

Strong hands gripped Crunnchu by the biceps and propelled him in front of the king. Crunnchu felt his heart sink as the king looked down sternly upon him and said, "So, your wife can beat my horses, eh? Now is that fact or is it the drink talking?"

Crunnchu wanted to take back the words, but once words are spoken they lie in the air until resolved, so he swallowed his fear and said, "Drink may have loosened my tongue, but facts is facts. My wife is swifter of foot than your horses' hooves."

"Then," the king said, "by all means bring this woman forward for a race!"

Crunnchu tried to slip away, but he was held fast as others went out to find his wife and bring her to the king's chair. They found her critically examining cloth at one of the stalls.

"Are you the wife of Crunnchu?" one asked.

She smiled. "Why, yes I am. What is it that you want?"

"We have come to bring you to your husband," another said, smirking and nudging his partner in the ribs with a broad elbow. "Seems like your husband's lips got to flapping and such that he insulted the king by claiming you were faster on your shapely toes than his horses could run." He ran his eye boldly up and down her and shook his head. "Ah then. 'Tis certain that I would never let me tongue run away with me thoughts if I had you in my bed."

"I see," she said politely, then raised her eyes to stare contemptuously into his own. He blinked and tried to meet them, but a hardness in their depths made him look away. "Go back and tell the king that my husband has spoken unwisely and it was not fitting for him to do so. As you can see, I can run no races, as I am with child."

The two looked down at her swelling belly as if they had not noticed it before and shook their heads.

"Sorry," the first said, "but if you don't come, why then the king will be obliged to take your husband's head. You see how it is, him being the one and all. I mean, well, a man can only take so much without—well—"

She sighed. "Then," she said lowly, "it appears that I must go with you."

Together they returned to the assembly, and everyone pushed against each other to see this woman who merited such rash words from her husband. She met their looks with disdain, then found herself in front of the king. "Why do you all look at me in this way? It is not seemly for you to stare at a woman in this condition. Why am I subjected to this rabble?" she asked the king.

"You will run against the king's horses!" a drunken man yelled from the multitude. "Aye, we'll see if your white heels can kick the dirt behind as quickly as your toes scrabble for the ceiling!"

A roar of laughter followed his words.

She shook her head. "This is foolishness," she snapped. "I cannot run a race as heavy with child as I am. My time is near."

The king smiled and shrugged and turned to the men standing beside him. "Well, then, since she won't run a race, take your swords and whack her husband's head off."

Her face turned white at his words, and she whirled to look at the crowd pressing tightly behind her. "Help me!" she cried to the warriors bearing arms. "In the names of the mothers who bore you, help me from this situation." None moved to help her, and she whirled to face the king again. "Then let the race be held after I am delivered of child. It will be only a short delay," she begged.

"No," the king said, lifting a goblet of wine and draining it. He tossed it to a serving-wench, who fumbled and caught it, breathing a silent sigh of relief and thanks for her quick hands. "Run the race."

Macha drew herself up proudly, her eyes flashing at all there. "Then the shame of what will happen will be upon the heads of all here who have shown such disrespect to me. A far greater weight will fall upon you for punishment!"

"What's this?" the king asked, frowning. "Who are you to speak in this way?"

"My name and the name of that I'll bear will forever be given to this place," she said. "I am Macha, daughter of Sainreth Mac Imbaith."[2] A swift intake of breath sounded audibly, as if the entire crowd had breathed at once. A shadow of uncertainty flickered over the king's face, but words will be words and—"Bring your horses forward," she said disdainfully.

In a flash she was off, her heels flying in a white blur behind her as the horses came next to her. The charioteer laid the goad to them but, strain as they did, they could not draw even with the running woman. She dashed across the finish well in front, but then a sudden scream shrieked from her lips and she fell to the ground, writhing in pain. A midwife rushed forward to help her, and she delivered twins, a son and daughter, before the horses reached the end of the race. That is why the Red Branch is called Emain Macha or Twins of Macha, and to this day it is called the same.

All the men who heard that cry of pain felt a weakness in their bellies, and they fell to their knees, having no more strength than a woman has in the midst of childbirth.

"From this hour," Macha said, raising her head and staring wrathfully at all there, "the insult you have given me will come again upon you to your shame. Whenever a threat comes to the borders of your land, all men shall feel as I feel now and know the pain I have felt as the weakness of a woman giving birth, and this shall remain upon you for five times five down through the fifth generation of the fifth generation, and it shall last for five [days and nights?]. Let it be so!"

And so it was. From the days of Crunnchu to the days of Fergus Mac Donnell and into the time of Forc Mac Dallan, son of Mainech, son of Lugaid, the men felt the pain in their bellies whenever the borders of their lands were threatened. Only three peoples escaped the curse of Macha: women, children, and Cúchulainn, who was not of Ulster. Only those men who left the province escaped the curse.

This, then, is the cause of the *Noinden Ulad,* the Pangs of the Ulstermen, the Red Branch warriors.

Notes

the story of cúchulainn's youth

1. *fidchell:* A game similar to chess.

2. The pangs of the Ulstermen came upon them whenever a foreign army crossed Ulster's borders. Since they had refused to intercede on Macha's behalf when Conchobor forced her to run a race against his horses while she was pregnant, Macha cursed them to feel birth pains when the men were needed most.

3. *ogham:* The early Irish alphabet formed by a series of slashes along a straight line.

cúchulainn's shield

1. Scáthach was considered the best trainer of warriors in the world. She did not take everyone, however, in her school in Alba or Scythia, depending upon the story being told.

the training of cúchulainn

1. The emphasis upon a year with each of the women suggests the old tradition of taking a wife for a year under the Brehon Laws. This would be a "contract marriage" only and the woman would not attain the right of "chief wife." Although women were, for the most part, awarded greater latitude in the Ancient Irish society than in other cultures, there were still restrictions placed upon them. They could, however, attain many positions on an equal status with men such as being judges, according to some of the old sagas and triads. I suspect that there is a conflict here and that women were given powers by *seanchis* who alluded to such rights being granted under the Brehon Laws. For those who would like to follow up on this, I can recommend *Land of Women* by Lisa M. Bitel (Cornell University Press, 1996).

2. The *gae bulga* was a spear that never missed its mark and was always fatal.

3. This is the first time we hear about Cúchulainn's travels. It would appear that this time is from an older version of the story that parallels the coming of the Tuatha De Danann, for it would explain how Cúchulainn attained the mystical weapon, the *gae bulga*.

the wooing of emer

1. *writh:* A rope-maker.

2. Translated by Randy Lee Eickhoff as *The Raid* (Forge Books, 1997).

3. *Iern-Gúal* appears to be translated as "Iron Coal" or "Iron-Charcoal." But *gúal* can be translated as "coal black" as well, as in a "coal black beverage," see *Ériu*, iv, 49.8, 61, *ngúal* translated as "the coal-hued drink," and a reference to a metal drinking vat in ZCP, viii, 65. I would suggest that the kettle is iron and the ale the men are drinking is a black ale.

4. *buanfach:* A game like checkers.

5. Lublochta Logo: The Gardens of Lugh. Now Lusk in County Dublin.

6. *Monach:* Guileful, tricky. This would suggest that Emer's father was a "trickster," implying a certain deceit that would not endear him to men.

7. Nemain's scarf: Nemain was a war goddess and wife of Néit who inspired battle madness with her scarf, which caused great confusion among armies.

8. *bodhran:* A drum made from a goatskin stretched over a frame. It is played with a double-knuckled stick held in one hand.

9. This is the beginning of a highly enigmatic word game between Cúchulainn and Emer.

10. This is one of the rare times when Cúchulainn acknowledges a deity as his father. We must remember that the story of Emer's courtship is a compilation of texts.

11. This isn't as odd a question as it seems, for the Brehon Laws allowed a man to have more than one wife and to have "contract wives" as well for a specified period of time. Emer's suggestion is that she would not be a second wife to anyone, which can also be inferred from the description she gives of herself.

12. Badb is part of the warrior triad, the Mórrígan. This is a pun on the name of Conchobor. There is a stream named Conchobor that joins the Dofolt.

13. This is a pun on his own name and how he came to be called the Hound of Culann.

14. Alba: Scotland.

15. Dornolla: Big-Fist. The suggestion is that she has large "knuckles" or "bumps" over her face.

16. Aengus: The love god.

17. In another version it is Forgall who sends the vision, making the other three homesick so they would return. If Cúchulainn returned without ful-

filling his journey, he would lose honor. And if he continued on the journey, he stood a better chance of being killed if he was alone.

18. This is a strange passage, for among all the foster fathers that Cúchulainn listed, Wulkin the Saxon was not included. According to an earlier passage, it was Cathbad, Sencha, and Amergin who taught Cúchulainn how to speak appropriately. We can assume by "sweet speech" the lady meant the Saxon language.

19. I suggest a lacuna here. It would seem that at one time there existed a passage where the young man recited Cúchulainn's future through the *imbas forasnai* ("the light of foresight"), but instead this recitation is given by Scáthach in the portion that has come to be known as *Verba Scáthaige*.

20. Some versions mention that warriors from Erin were already there studying under Scáthach. They were Ferdiad, son of Damán, whom Cúchulainn will fight in the famous duel at the ford in *Táin Bó Cuailngé*; and Naisi, son of Usneach, who will marry Deirdre and become a part of "the three sorrows of storytelling." Loch Mór, son of Egomas, and Fiamain, son of Fora, were also there.

21. Scáthach's name means "fear," while her daughter's name means "terrible." Thus, the initiation that will admit Cúchulainn to manhood is an amorous one with the daughter and a sexual one with the mother. See *The Training of Cúchulainn* for another account of this.

22. This is another inconsistency in the story; we are aware that in Part I Cúchulainn had promised Emer that he would remain chaste as long as he was away from her and would not wed another.

23. The *imbas forasnai* is a pagan ritual that was practiced by the prophets or seers in order to acquire supernatural knowledge. The vision they received after chewing a piece of raw animal flesh and chanting an incantation would sometimes be referred to as the *imbas forasnai,* suggesting this was a particular and only vision. It was not. It simply refers to the *last* time the individual experienced such a thing and, at times, simply to the ability to look into the future.

24. The Fomorians lived under or upon the sea. They were the evil gods of Irish myth, misshapen and violent. Their center appears to have been Tory Island. They are often shown as having one hand, one foot, or one eye. They were defeated for all time at the Second Battle of Mag Tuireadh.

25. The reference here is to the practice among the Ancient Irish of contracting for one year for a wife. This was allowed under the Brehon Laws, and no shame was attached to it. This is an oddity in the story, however, as Cúchulainn has always said that he could not marry a woman who was

not a virgin and Emer had told him that she would be a second wife to no one.

26. Loch Cuan: Strangford Lough.

27. This is taken from *The Story of Derbforgaille,* which contradicts part of this story. By tasting her blood, he had made her part of his clan, and any marriage within a clan was forbidden as incest.

28. This is the famous *carpat serrda,* scythed chariot.

29. *glond:* Deed, but especially a worthy deed.

30. Raeban: White Hill.

31. This is an ancient custom in which the "king's right" was linked to a union that existed between the king and the land. The sacrifice of a woman's virginity represented a unification of the king and the land and ensured that good fortune would continue throughout the land. The woman becomes the symbolic earth, thus "marrying" the king to her through the first "plowing of the field" to ensure the fertility of the earth. Psychoanalytically, this is recognized as the junction of Eros and Thanatos as the woman gives to the man not her whole self but only that part of her which is the orgasmic joy. Yet she cannot help but be transformed (she is no longer a virgin) and becomes the woman whose field is ready for bearing.

cúchulainn and fedelm

1. *Imbas forasnai* is the name of an ancient divination ritual, perhaps best translated as "illumination between the hands." The diviner first chewed raw animal flesh, then spoke an incantation over his hands and placed them over his cheeks. Whatever had remained hidden from view or from thought was then revealed, usually in a dream. For more information, see "Imbas Forasnai" by Nora K. Chadwick, in *Scottish Gaelic Studies,* vol. 4 (Oxford University Press, 1935).

2. Foltcháin: "Of the lovely hair."

3. According to the Brehon Laws, all individuals had a "blush price" that had to be paid if they were insulted and not compensated for this insult to their honor. The suggestion here is that the "punishment" levied upon Fedelm was exorbitant and was responsible for the "curse" being settled upon the men for not helping to stop this indignity. This, however, is a problematic interpretation as the one who should have been punished was Cúchulainn, but he was not from Ulster.

the cattle raid of regamna

1. Ath da Ferta: Ford of the Two Chariot Poles.

2. This is a description of the Mórrígan, part of the war goddess triune. The other two are Macha and Badb.

3. The hazel tree allegedly has magical properties and is associated with sorcery and witchcraft.

4. Cúchulainn is referring to the fact that, as the champion of Ulster, he is responsible for all of the cattle within its borders.

5. A satirist was a person to be feared, for he or she could make a poem that would damage a person forever. A few satirists were so powerful that they could raise blemishes, cripple people, and in some cases even cause their deaths.

6. In *The Cattle Raid of Cooley,* Dáire owns the Donn Cuailngé, the Brown Bull sought by Maeve.

7. *grellach:* Clayey place.

8. *dolluid:* Enchanted place.

9. *fir fer:* "We shall know the truth then" is probably the intent, although the phrase can refer to faithfulness of men, truth of men, or the good of a warrior's honor.

cúchulainn and senbecc

1. *timpán:* A musical instrument.

2. The manuscript abruptly ends here.

3. These are the names of the nine hazels: Sall, Fall, Fuball, Finnam, Fonnam, Fofuigell, Crú, Crínam, Cruanbla.

the wasting sickness of cúchulainn *and* the only jealousy of emer

1. Cúchulainn's wife is referred to as Ethne Ingubai here, but later becomes Emer. The suggestion is that this part of the story might be an older account that predates *Tochmarc Emire, The Wooing of Emer,* in which Cúchulainn gains his wife. We might also assume, however, that Ethne is a "one-year wife" or a woman who has agreed to be a second wife to Cúchulainn for one year. This does, however, contradict a statement Cúchulainn makes to Emer when he is courting her; he says that he will not take any woman as wife who has slept with another man. Of course, Cúchulainn might have been the first woman that Ethne slept with, but this seems an arguable question best solved in other forms.

2. Although blemishes are punishable under the Brehon Laws, they are also divided into intentional and unintentional categories, and a fine dis-

tinction is made in the awarding of payment. Leborcham is suggesting that Cúchulainn's very appearance is so striking that the women of Ulster are hurt by his presence and, therefore, he owes them some compensation for causing them this "discomfort." But he was not the only warrior responsible for causing them some "distress," as is pointed out. It is curious that Cúchulainn allows himself to be convinced by this argument and gathers the birds as a compensation for having caused the women of Ulster their grief of blemish when logically he was free from having caused any intentional harm.

3. The two horses that pulled Cúchulainn's chariot were magical and had disappeared for three hundred years before Cúchulainn's birth. When Cúchulainn took his arms, they reappeared, but Cúchulainn had to prove he was worthy of them. He rode each for a full day and night all over Ireland as they tried to throw him. When they could not, they became his horses, and only he and Laeg could handle them.

4. The names here are a key to the mystical world into which Cúchulainn will be traveling. Manannan is the son of the sea or the "sea god." Lúathlám ar Cladeb means "Swift Sword-Weilder." Mag Mell is the Plain of Delight.

5. This story can be found in Randy Lee Eickhoff, *The Destruction of the Inn* (Forge Books, 2001).

appendix c: the pangs of the ulstermen

1. In this instance, we assume that Crunnchu has a "contract wife," one without the formality of ceremony that usually would follow the taking of another main wife. For that purpose I will refer to her as his wife throughout the rest of the story.

2. His name means "strange (or weird) son of the seas."